For Aiden and Caleb,
who wait patiently for a dog of their own.

To Emai,
Happy reading!
Amber Byers

ISBN: 978-1-7328286-0-5

Library of Congress Control Number: 2018910829

Cover Illustration by Penny Weber
Cover Design by Patty Kelly

Tadpole Press
Lafayette, Colorado

www.tadpolepress.com
www.amberbyersblog.blogspot.com

First Edition
Printed in the United States of America

Chapter 1

Tomorrow is the first day of third grade, and I am so excited! I already found out that Nadine is in my class. Nadine is one of my best friends, and she lives down the street. We both have Colby as our teacher this year. We weren't in the same class last year, so I know this year is going to be great.

Papa and I went back-to-school shopping last week, and now Daddy and I are sitting on my bedroom floor double-checking the list of school supplies. I put one pencil with tiny dogs printed on it into my backpack just for me. The rest of the school supplies to share with the class go into another bag.

"I can't believe my little girl is going to third grade already," Daddy says. I smile. I know he is happy, even though I see tears sparkling at the corners of his eyes.

"Do you like the notebook I picked out?" I ask him. It has a picture of a dog on the front.

"Yes, it's great. It's totally you," he responds and smiles back.

Anything I pick out usually has dogs on it. They are my absolute favorite thing. I think they are one of the coolest animals ever. We have two cats—a black one named Artemis and a gray one named Orion—and I love them both. I love when they sleep on my bed or curl up on the couch next to me. I love when they chase a toy mouse around the house and hop up on their back paws to pounce on it. Even though I love them so much, I still really want a dog to chase sticks, play fetch, and go for a walk with.

Papa says when I was little, I tied a string onto Orion's collar and tried to take him for a walk outside. We made it all the way to the front sidewalk where Orion laid down in the sun and licked himself. When I tried to pick him up to make him walk, he scratched me and ran back inside.

Daddy says when Artemis was a kitten, she used to play catch with a little ball. Daddy would throw it down the hallway, and Artemis would happily run after it, pick it up with her teeth, and jog it dutifully back to him. But that was a long time ago, and our kitties are getting older so they're not as interested in that now.

* * *

When I wake up in the morning, Daddy has already left for work. He works with computers and sometimes he works so much that I don't see him when I wake up or before I go to bed.

My stomach is full of butterflies as I brush my teeth and comb my hair. I run downstairs and climb into my booster seat while Papa loads up the school supplies in the car.

As we drive, I wonder what my teacher, Colby, will be like and who else will be in my class. Papa parks and as soon as I climb out of the car, I run over to see my friends. We chatter excitedly as we walk inside. When I get to the classroom door, I turn around and see Papa following behind, carrying the bag of school supplies. Nadine is already in the classroom. She gives me a big hug and Papa takes a picture of us.

"You two have grown so much!" he gushes, then gives us both big hugs, and kisses me on the top of my head. I wave as he leaves, feeling like this will be a good year.

* * *

It turns out that my new teacher, Colby, is really funny. The first thing he does is tell a joke.

"Knock, knock."

"Who's there?" we all respond together.

"Lettuce."

"Lettuce who?" we shout.

"Lettuce in, it's cold out here!" he says with a grin, and everyone laughs.

Right after breakfast, we have math time. Math time is my favorite because of Maddie, the math dog. Maddie is this sweet yellow Lab who visits all of the classes during math time. Magnolia brings Maddie in and announces that she has learned a few new tricks over the summer. Meanwhile, Maddie lumbers around the classroom, placing her head or paw on each student's lap as if to say, *It's good to see you again, my friend.* Everyone loves Maddie, even Emery, who used to be afraid of dogs. Because Maddie is so calm and well-behaved, it's easy to get over your fears. Not that I've ever been afraid of dogs.

"Today we're going to do math outside and Magnolia will show us the new counting trick that Maddie learned over the summer," our teacher, Colby, explains.

We line up and follow Maddie to the field by the playground. I plop down onto my knees and sit in the soft, green grass.

Magnolia commands Maddie to sit, then holds a ball up and says, "One." Maddie watches as Magnolia throws the ball across the field.

Magnolia reaches down and picks up another ball, holding it for Maddie to see. "Two." Maddie watches again as Magnolia throws the second ball across the field.

Magnolia then reaches down a third time and holds this ball out for Maddie to see. "Three." Maddie watches as Magnolia throws the third ball across the field.

Finally, Magnolia shouts, "One, Maddie! Go get it!" And Maddie tears across the field, picks up the first ball with her mouth, and runs back.

"Good dog, Maddie, good dog!" Magnolia tells her as she pets Maddie's head. "Two, Maddie! Go get it!"

Maddie drops the ball from her mouth and races across the field toward the second ball, then returns and drops the ball.

"Three! Go get it, Maddie!" Magnolia shouts.

Maddie turns and sprints back across the field toward the last ball, picks it up, and speeds back.

"Good dog, Maddie!" Magnolia praises her, then adds, "Four! Go get it!"

Magnolia stands with her arm out, pointing to the field, but Maddie sits down and cocks her head to the side with a puzzled look on her face as if to say, *Why are you asking me to do this a fourth time? You said we were only counting to three.* Magnolia kneels down, rubs her ears, and tells her, "Good dog, Maddie. Good dog."

Magnolia turns to us and says, "Did you see how Maddie counted to three?"

We all nod.

"She didn't run a fourth time when I told her to because she remembered that I had only thrown three balls," Magnolia continues.

Maddie lies down and starts chewing one of the balls.

"Do you think you're ready to do some math now, class?" Magnolia asks.

"Yes!" we chorus. I figure if Maddie can do it—even if she only counted to three—then I can be good at math too.

Colby arranges us into small groups and tells us to turn to page seven in our math notebooks. I can't stand it and I have to run up to Maddie and give her a quick hug. I place my arms around her neck and feel her velvety smooth fur rub against my cheek. Then I sit back down in the grass with my small group, pick up my pencil, and balance my notebook on my knee.

As we go through the lesson, Maddie ambles around, stopping to sit next to students. I feel like she's listening and learning right along with me, getting the skills she needs to learn her next trick. When she comes over to my group, she plops her head right down in the middle of my lap and makes these contented little breathing noises as I stroke her ears. After a minute, I think she may have dozed off because her eyes are closed and it sounds like she is snoring. I could do math like this all day.

* * *

At writing time, we read a story about a frog who wanted to grow up and become a princess. Colby tells us to draw a picture or write something to show our connection to the story.

First, I draw a frog. Then I add a crown to show that he became a princess. I think about how I connect to the story. I saw a frog once down by the creek. Some of the kids in my class are always playing princess and would love to have a crown. But I think the story is about more than frogs and princesses. I think it is about really wanting something, deep down, even if it seems impossible. Immediately, I know my connection.

I begin by drawing a picture of me with my curly, brown hair and a big smile on my face. Then I draw a picture of a dog next to me. It is little and mostly white, with cute black spots all over it. I want to have a dog more than anything. Papa says dogs take a lot of time, and Daddy says they don't have enough time to deal with a dog right now. When I am finished with my picture, I write all the reasons why I want a dog.

They give you company.
They are furry.
They are fun to play with.
We can play fetch and go for walks.
They will like the cats.

I smile. Just thinking about dogs makes me happy. Writing time isn't over yet, so I go over to the reading corner and pick out a book about a dog. I am completely sucked into the book when Colby says it's lunchtime. I carefully put the book away and join the rest of the class in line.

For lunch today, I have a veggie pita with hummus. I love hummus. It is turning out to be a great day. Nadine and I sit next to Tino and Emery. Tino is telling us about how he got to go to Florida this summer. He went on a boat and saw real dolphins diving in the water.

Emery exclaims, "I love dolphins! They're my favorite!" Then he adds, "I didn't go anywhere. We just stayed here, but I did go swimming a lot. I can even jump off the diving board now."

At recess after lunch, it's so hot outside that it still feels like summer. Nadine and I race each other to the swings and sail up as high as we can in the air. The breeze cools me down, and I feel like I am flying, floating, full of all the excitement and hope in the world. I hope the whole year will be this amazing.

* * *

When we get back inside, it's library time. The library is one of my favorite places to be. The bookshelves tower over me, stacked so full of books that they seem to reach to the sky. Hanging from the ceiling is a huge papier-mâché dragon that snakes across the ceiling from one end of the room to the other. There is even fire coming out of

7

its mouth. It is so cool.

Real trees grow out of pots in the corners of the room, and vines curl around the trees and spread out across the ceiling so it feels like we're in a jungle. Hanging down from the ceiling between the vines are beautiful clouds cut out of large poster boards and painted shades of gray, silver, and blue. Posters on the wall say things like "Keep on Reading," "The Best Things in Life Can Be Found in a Book," and "Books Are Everywhere." Every time I come in, I feel so happy to be here.

Everyone sits down on the middle of the rug and leans back against the pillows that are arranged in a circle on the floor. We listen to the librarian, Aldo, read *The Name Jar*. It's about a girl who moves from Korea to America. On her first day of school, no one can pronounce her name, Unhei, and she worries that she should change it. But her name is special and reminds her of her grandma. By the end of the week, she decides to keep it and help teach everyone how to say it correctly.

Aldo asks us to say it, so we all chant in unison, "Yoon-hye!"

Then he asks if we know where Korea is. "I do!" Emery shouts, raising his hand. "Our neighbor's mom moved here from Korea and she said it's all the way on the other side of the world."

"Good, yes, that's true," Aldo responds. We gather around the globe as Aldo spins it all the way across the Pacific Ocean and points to a small country surrounded by water. I wonder what it would be like to live around that much water. I live in Colorado where there aren't any oceans. But my city, Lafayette, does have a small lake called Waneka Lake. It is one of my favorite places in the world.

When we're free to wander around the library to choose our own book to take home, I keep thinking about all of the changes that Unhei went through, from moving across the world to starting a new school and learning a new language. I am so glad that I'm not starting a new school where I would have to make new friends all over again. But it would be fun to learn a new language and see what the other side of the world looks like.

I'm glad Unhei didn't change her name. It has such a special meaning and is a big part of who she is. And it's really unique. Sophie isn't really unique, so I don't have the same problem of people not being able to pronounce it. Everyone seems to know that the *ph* in it sounds like an *f*. Our language is funny that way; you write it one way and say it another. I play around with my name in my head. What if it was said Sop-hye, so it rhymed with Unhei? Though Unhei's name ended with *h-e-i* and mine is *h-i-e*.

"What are you doing?" I hear a voice and look up to see someone staring at me through the bookshelf. It's Nadine.

"Oh, was I talking out loud?" I ask. I must have been and I didn't even know it.

"Um, yeah. Something about a mop?" Nadine guesses.

"Oh, I was just saying my name different ways. Like 'Sop-hye'." Now that I say it out loud, it does seem kind of silly, and I try not to laugh because we're still in the library. But I can't quite manage it and before long, Nadine is over on my side of the bookshelf and we're both bent over double with giggles, gasping for air.

Aldo walks down the aisle toward us, shaking his head, but I can tell he is trying not to smile so I know he's not too mad. Library time is almost over, so I take a deep breath to calm down and pull *Jake* from The Puppy Place series off the shelf. Nadine and I try to pull ourselves together so we're not laughing like crazy as we walk down the hallway to art.

Somehow we manage, though not without one more burst of giggles when Nadine whispers behind me, "Green bean Nadine."

I don't know why it's even funny since it's just a simple rhyme, but that's the way Nadine is. She is always making me laugh.

* * *

In art class, we get to paint. On the first day! No lectures about respecting materials or keeping things clean.

Our art teacher, Rosa, pulls her long, black hair into a ponytail and turns on some salsa music.

"Welcome back to school, dears!" she says with a big smile. "Grab an apron! It's the first day back, so we're starting our creative engines, getting our juices flowing again."

Then she opens the bottles of paint, pours them onto each palette, and bounces around the room as the music plays.

Everyone is smiling as Rosa dances around the room, checking on our work. Sometimes Rosa stops and claps her hands together or exclaims, "Ooh, how lovely!"

Nadine has painted a big *N* on her paper with little flowers and hearts all around it.

I am painting a house with me, Daddy, Papa, Artemis, and Orion standing outside even though Artemis and Orion aren't allowed to go outside. Then I paint a big heart right across the front door, because that's what my house looks like to me.

Suddenly, I hear a *crash!* and everyone whirls around to see Tino with a scared look on his face and paint dripping down his apron into a puddle. The blues are blending into the reds, making a deep purple that spreads across the floor. He looks like he might start crying, but Rosa breezes over to him, rubs his back, and says, "That's what aprons are for, my dear."

In an instant, Rosa and Tino have cleaned the paint up off the floor and gotten all of the globs off Tino's apron. The only parts they can't clean are Tino's shoes. His shoelaces have turned a deep shade of violet.

"Not to worry," Rosa reassures him. "Those shoes look quite stunning with a touch of purple. That's what we call a beautiful oops."

And with that, we all clean up our stations and Rosa sends us back to our classroom to gather our things for the end of the day. When the bell rings, I squeeze my way through the crowd of students filling the hallways, all trying to leave at the same time. As I step outside onto the playground, the bright sun blinds my eyes momentarily. I hold my hand up to shield my eyes and see Papa's dark, wavy hair through the crowd. I rush into his arms, and he gives me a big squeeze.

I immediately start talking. "You wouldn't believe it! We had the best day ever! Colby is super funny and Maddie is the sweetest dog and we had hummus for lunch and I flew so high on the swings and Aldo read the best book ever and you should have seen Tino's shoes, it was a mess but now he has purple shoelaces! May I have purple shoelaces, please???"

"Whoa there, turbo," Papa responds. "I don't think I got all that, but it sounds like you like third grade?"

"It's the best in the world! And did I tell you Colby is sooo funny? Though not as funny as Nadine," I answer and suppress another fit of giggles.

"Well, tell you what. We have some extra time before we have to head home and get dinner ready, so you get to choose if we stop by Waneka Lake or head straight home for a walk by the creek."

"Waneka Lake!" I shout, jumping up and down.

"Waneka Lake it is then," he says.

When we get to the lake, I jump out of the car and skip across the grass, past the playground, and onto the beach. This is one of my favorite places in the whole world. I dig around in the sand and mud for a bit, then toss bits of twigs and little pebbles into the water. When I get bored with that, I draw my name in the sand with a stick and circle it with a heart.

When I was adopted, Daddy and Papa didn't change my name. Well, they didn't change my first name, but they did change my last name. It used to be Duncan. Sophie Olivia Duncan. Now it's Sophie Olivia Granbould, and now we all match.

Daddy's last name used to be Granville and Papa's last name used to be Archibould, so when they got married, they took the first part of Daddy's name and the last part of Papa's name to make Granbould. They could have done Archiville, but they didn't like that as much. So now I'm a Granbould too. I like that our name is something special that could have only been created with Daddy and Papa. So even though I don't have a very unique first name, I don't know anyone else with my same last name except for my Daddy and Papa.

"Papa, did you ever think about changing my name when I was adopted?" I ask.

"Well, we had a few names that we had talked about before we met you, but we could never agree on one," he says with a laugh. "Plus, you were a month old when we adopted you and your birth parents had already chosen your name. We all talked about it and decided it was a beautiful gift that you could keep from them."

I nod and think it over for a minute. "That's what I would have chosen too," I say. I can't imagine having any other name.

Chapter 2

"Daddy, may I play at Nadine's house?" I ask.

It is Saturday afternoon and Daddy is working in his office. "Did you finish your chores?" he asks, not looking up.

"Yes."

He turns to me and asks, "All the way?"

I nod and watch as Daddy types something, then closes his laptop with a click. He sighs and runs his finger over the rainbow sticker that has been on the lid of his laptop for so long that it's beginning to peel off. Then he looks up and declares, "Let's go see how your room looks."

I follow him into my bedroom where clothes are strewn about on the floor, mixed together with books and pencils and art projects I'm working on.

"Ooh, look, I forgot about these!" I say, pulling an apple-head doll out from under a sweater crumpled on the floor. I hold it out to show Daddy. "See how I carved a little face on a crab apple from our backyard and stuck it on this popsicle stick? Isn't it cool? I have a whole family of them somewhere . . ."

Daddy runs his hand through his straight, blond hair and shakes his head. "Clean up everything on your floor and then you may go," he says and goes back into his office.

I quickly grab the books and set them in a stack on the bookshelf. Then I collect all of the pencils and art supplies and pile them together in a heap. Next I grab all of the clothes and dump them into my laundry basket. I find the rest of my apple-head dolls at the bottom of the pile of clothes and set them on my bed.

"I'm done!" I shout as I run down the hallway. "May I go now please?"

"Yes, you may run down and see if she's home. But come straight back and let me know if you're staying. And come straight back if you're not staying. Got it?" he answers.

"Yep, thanks!" I say and hurriedly jam my feet into my shoes.

"Okay, what do you do if she invites you in?" Daddy quizzes me, following me to our front door. Nadine and I live in the same row of townhomes, so she's really close and I don't even have to cross a street to get to her house. It's practically the only place I'm allowed to go outside on my own.

"I come back and tell you," I answer dutifully.

"Good," he responds and questions again, "Now, what do you do if she's not there or you can't play?"

"Come back and tell you," I say, hopping on one foot with excitement.

"Okay, good. Have fun, sweet pea," he says, bending down to kiss the top of my head.

I run out the door and down the steps, skidding as I zip around the corner. Five houses later and I'm knocking on Nadine's door. Her mom answers and three dogs and a toddler suction themselves to the back of her legs as she tries to keep them all inside. "Sophie! Come on in, but quickly please. I have a torrent of energy and excitement that is trying to escape out the front door."

"Okay," I say and step inside. "May I play with Nadine?"

"Yes, of course. She's upstairs in her room," she says to me, then shouts upstairs, "Nadine! Sophie's here!"

"I have to tell my dad that I can stay first," I say, apologizing as I squeeze back out the door, trying not to let the torrent—as she called it—out.

Outside, I run down the block back to our house and crash open the door. "Daddy! I'm staying!" I shout from the doorway. He comes into the hallway, ties my shoelaces that have come undone, and tells me, "Be back home by four o'clock, please."

"Okay," I say as I dash back outside.

Before I'm even at the end of the steps, I see Nadine running toward my house. As I catch up to her, she spins around and we sprint back to her house and up the stairs to her bedroom. All three of her dogs follow us into her bedroom, wagging their tails.

The biggest one—a black, curly-haired dog named Patch—nearly knocks me over with his excitement, but I don't mind. The smallest one—an adorable, tiny, white puppy named Luna—jumps as high as she can and practically lands on top of Patch's head, knocking both dogs over in an excited heap. The third one—a calmer, light brown Lab named Ginger—dances a few circles around them, then settles down right in the middle. We laugh and sit down to pet them, rubbing their ears and bellies until they finally calm down.

"You are so lucky," I tell Nadine. "It's always so exciting at your house."

"Yeah, but sometimes it's a little too loud. Pia is always crying and taking everyone's attention, and I have to do all the grown-up things."

I think about that and wonder if I would feel the same way if I had a little sister. Mostly though, I still think she's lucky as I lie down on the floor and lean my head up against Ginger's big, smooth belly. She wags her tail happily, and I scratch her ears.

"Sometimes I wish I had a frog for a pet instead," she confides. "They're so quiet."

I laugh at that, but then I think she's crazy. Dogs are so soft and cuddly, and my house is quiet enough since I'm the only kid. I wish more than anything that I had my own dog. And Nadine has three! I wish I could have three dogs to greet me every time I came home. But at least I can come over to her house and play with them all the time. When her family goes out of town, we take care of the dogs, which is a lot of fun.

"Don't you remember before Pia was born and you really wanted a baby sister?" I ask, looking at the frown on Nadine's face.

"Yeah . . . that seems like a long time ago, though," she says. "Before Pia was born, Mommy and Daddy used to be able to listen to me all the time. Now I have to shout just to get heard."

"It doesn't sound like it's the dogs' fault to me," I say. I can hardly imagine anything that would be a dog's fault. "And Pia didn't always used to cry and scream that much. Remember how cute she was when she was a baby and she would wrap her tiny, little baby hands around our fingers?" Nadine smiles. "Yeah, that was pretty great. And you're right, she wasn't always this loud. But now she runs around and steals my toys and pulls the dogs' tails, and nobody can hear anything over all the screaming and barking. But," she adds, looking at me, "you seem to have calmed the dogs down."

I smile. Nadine's right. The dogs are all curled around me on the floor, gazing at me lazily through half open eyes.

* * *

We talk and play all afternoon until it's time to go home. I pet all of the dogs one last time, give Nadine a hug, and squeeze out the door, making sure that none of the dogs escape.

As soon as I walk in my house, I call out, "I'm home! Can I get a puppy?" I am always asking for a puppy. Or a dog. But the answer has always been no.

Papa has said we will get one eventually, just not right now. And Daddy has said if I really want a dog, then I should do a good job and help out with the chores to show him that I'm responsible enough. So I do. I try really hard to do a good job. Every time I put away my clothes and pick up my toys, I picture that puppy in my head.

"Welcome home, darling. And no, you can't have a

puppy, but you can come cook dinner with me," Papa says from the kitchen.

* * *

On Monday, we bike to Louisville for the Labor Day parade. It's hot outside again, so I am wearing shorts and a red, white, and blue striped shirt with a big blue star in the middle. Papa smears sunscreen on my face, arms, and neck, and then hands me my sunglasses and helmet.

We bike along the Coal Creek trail. Sunshine dances through the leaves onto the path, and I can hear water bubbling as it flows down the creek. After a few minutes, we pull to the side and stop. Daddy sits on a tree trunk that is lying sideways on the ground, knocked down from the flood we had a few years ago.

"Better have a sip now before we head up the hill," he tells me, handing me a water bottle from his backpack.

As I drink, I watch prairie dogs emerge from their underground homes in the field next to the creek. Even though they're called dogs, I think they look more like squirrels. At first, they cautiously stick their noses in the air, then some climb out of their holes and nibble on the grass.

I hand my water bottle back to Daddy and walk closer to the prairie dog homes. Several prairie dogs stand up on their back legs and wag their tails. Another biker flies down the trail, and the prairie dogs chirp loudly to each other and quickly dive back down into their holes.

"Did you know that prairie dogs have a language just

like we do?" Papa asks, walking over toward me.

"Really?" I ask without looking up.

Daddy joins us and responds, "Yeah, they have different sounds to warn for different predators."

"You mean like their chirping?" I ask, kneeling down to peer into one of the holes.

"Yeah, they use different chirps and barks to tell the rest of the group what to look out for. Like that biker, or a coyote, or you," Daddy adds, watching me crouch down.

"That is so cool," I say, standing up. "I wish I could speak prairie dog language."

We hop back on our bikes and pedal past the prairie dog homes up the hill. Pretty soon, I have to get off and walk. I catch my breath at the top, feeling the sun beating down on my skin. Coasting down the other side of the hill into Louisville, the wind blows over my skin and cools me down. I keep my eyes focused on the trail, careful not to get too close to the edge or turn too fast in the loose gravel.

At the park, I hop off my bike and run over to the playground where Nadine is climbing the jungle gym and Pia is playing in the sand.

"Hey, watch this!" Nadine calls, as she loops herself down between the monkey bars and starts swinging her way across.

"Watch me now!" I say and hop up, swinging easily across.

"Pia! Don't put that in your mouth!" I hear Nadine's mom shout, and I look down to see Pia trying to eat a rock. Or a bug, I can't tell.

I reach for the last bar, but my hand slips and I crash down to the ground. My knee smashes into the metal pole and my palms scrape along the woodchips lining the ground. "Oweeeee!" I wail.

Papa rushes over and pulls me onto his lap in one big swoop. Just being in his arms makes me feel a little bit safer, but my knee and my hands still hurt and tears spill down my cheeks. Daddy reaches into his backpack for the first aid kit, then pulls out a wet wipe. He wipes my hands clean, puts a Band-Aid on each one, then kisses both hands. Then he bends down and kisses my knee. Instantly, as if his kisses were magic medicine, I feel better.

They each give me one more squeeze and I hop off Papa's lap as Emery arrives. "Cool, you have Nemo *and* Star Wars Band-Aids! What did you do, rip off your whole hand?" he says when he sees me.

I laugh, but his mom says, "Emery!" in that voice that parents use that means they don't like something we did. I see her shake her head as we run off to the frog pond.

Before we even get all the way there, frogs start jumping into the water. *Plop. Plop. Plop.* I didn't even see them sitting in the grass before they jumped. Five, six, seven. Four more. Twelve, thirteen, fourteen. There are so many I can't even count. The whole pond is covered in bright green algae, and cattails grow along the side.

Emery has brought a little net like the kind you use to try to catch tadpoles or butterflies and he has this look of determination on his face that says he's for real.

"Gotcha!" he shouts, slamming the net down on the

bank. But when he lifts it up, there's nothing underneath.

As we walk around the pond, we take turns using Emery's net to try again and again to catch a frog. Nadine swishes too fast and misses. I see three frogs sitting close together and decide I can get at least one of them, but my net lands in the middle and I don't get any. Every time we take a step, more frogs splash into the water. Pretty soon, the whole pond is rimmed with tiny pairs of bulging, green eyes sticking out of the algae-covered surface.

One frog sits in the water near the bank, its back a brownish-green bump barely visible through the algae. It's Emery's turn again, and he slowly creeps toward it. We hold our breath. This could be it. Less than a foot away, he swings the net down right over the frog and . . . *splash!* Emery falls into the pond! "Ahhhh!" he shrieks and frantically starts waving his arms. The net goes flying and suddenly algae, water, mud, and Emery are churning about in a huge, noisy ruckus.

His mom and dad come running, but fortunately the pond isn't too deep and he's able to pull himself to the side and cling to the slippery shore before they get there.

"Emery! What on earth?! Are you okay?" They drag him the rest of the way out, and he is smiling from ear to ear. Dark, wet mud clings to the bottom half of his body and face, and slimy, green algae sticks to him everywhere. There's a pile of it on his head, down his neck, covering his clothes, and down to his feet, even turning one white sock bright green. *Wait, a sock? Wasn't he wearing shoes when we were walking around?*

His mom seems to notice at the same time and a frown creases her face as though a cloud just covered the sun. "Emerson Magby . . . where is your shoe?"

But Emery is already talking. "Did I get the frog?!" he asks hopefully.

"Emery, your shoe," his mom reminds him.

"Uh . . . yeah, it must have gotten stuck in the mud when I crawled out. The whole bottom of the pond feels like goo!" he responds excitedly. "I'll go get it."

Nadine spies the net several feet away on the bank. We go over to get it while Emery steps back in to get his missing shoe. Before Nadine even picks up the net, we know it is empty. Bad luck, I thought for sure he'd get it that time. In all the commotion, the frogs must have retreated to the other side of the pond for safety, because we don't see them jumping anymore.

Emery's dad is now trying to hold onto him to help pull him out, though it looks like he doesn't really want to touch him. Emery emerges with what could be his shoe or a lumpy, muddy, black-coated blob covered in algae.

Nadine hands Emery the net and he drops the lump into the net and bobs it up and down a couple of times in the water to try to clean it up, but he stirred up so much mud that the water here doesn't look much cleaner than the shoe. After a few more bobs up and down in the water, the lump starts to resemble a shoe and his mom says that's about as clean as he's going to get it so he might as well come out before he falls back in again.

Pia is here now, too, and points at the lump in the net,

saying, "Frog, Mommy! Frog!"

Emery dumps water out of his shoe and hurriedly puts it back on, beaming.

I pick a cattail and playfully bat Nadine with it. Each time the cattail hits her, white seed puffs explode out of the brown part of the plant. Nadine and Emery join in and pretty soon, we all have white, fluffy stuff stuck to us everywhere.

Daddy tells us it's time to go and the grown-ups have a quick discussion about Emery. There's not much to do for Emery's clothes since no one has any extras and the parade is starting soon. Emery assures his parents that he doesn't mind and besides, he'll dry off in the sun. "Maybe people will think I've dressed up for the parade as a swamp monster!" he says eagerly. "Maybe I can even join one of the floats!"

"You will absolutely not be climbing on any of the floats," his mom says firmly, "and please try not to touch anyone either."

But his parents relent and agree that he can go to the parade as he is. As we walk, his shoes make a *squish, squish* sound every time he steps. Big, white cattail fluff floats in the air above the muddy footprints behind us.

We choose a place near the end of the parade that's the least crowded we can find so Emery doesn't smear his mud all over people trying to squeeze in with the crowd. It turns out our shady little place away from the crowd is the perfect place to watch. First is the pet parade, and when the kids finish marching their pets through the parade, they end up right in front of us. Daddy says he doesn't think our cats would like the parade, but whenever I get a dog, I want to walk it in the pet parade.

Most kids have brought dogs, though there are a few rabbits, a guinea pig, and even a turtle. A lot of them are dressed up too. We see kids and pets dressed up in matching princess and superhero costumes, but Emery is still the only swamp monster.

Chapter 3

At school the next week, we are learning about animal habitats in science class. Our teacher, Colby, tells us that a habitat is an animal's home or place where it lives. He also explains how some animals thrive in certain types of places. Like how polar bears live where it is really cold, and sharks live in deep water in the ocean.

Then he asks Nadine to hand out paper cutouts of all kinds of different animals to the class, and we each get to attach them to the right habitat poster on the wall. I have a snake, a sea star, and a coyote. I know right away that the sea star lives in water, so I stick that cutout on the ocean habitat poster. There are already some snakes on the rain forest and desert habitat posters, so I put mine on the rain forest poster.

Next I look down at the coyote cutout. Daddy and Papa have said that they hear coyotes howling at night sometimes, especially in the summer. So I know that there are coyotes close to our house, but I'm not sure what our habitat is, so I guess and put the last cutout on the mountains habitat poster since we live near the mountains.

Even though I like school, I feel like there is so much to learn that my brain is already filling up. It makes me feel tired. Maybe it is just a hard day.

* * *

We have P.E. class next. Since it is still so warm, we

get to have class outside. Our gym teacher, Ping, leads us outside to the soccer field where we do jumping jacks and stretches to get warmed up. Then we break off into teams to play soccer. Some kids are really good at it, but I'm only okay. I like when I get to use my hands to throw the ball back onto the field when it goes out of bounds, but when I have to kick it, my feet get all tangled up.

Eventually, we take a break and sit down on the grass to drink some water. Nadine sets her water bottle to the side, lies back in the grass, and looks dreamily up at the clouds. I flop down next to her and we lie there quietly for a while, catching our breath. The breeze floats gently over us, barely enough to cool our skin and rustle our hair.

"Want to play at the creek today after school?" she asks.

"Yeah, I'll ask my dad," I say happily. "Can the dogs come?" They are so fun to watch as they romp in and out of the water.

"Sure, I'll ask," she replies.

It's nice that Nadine lives so close to me. Sometimes it feels like she's my sister and we're part of the same family. I like her loud, busy family and sometimes she likes to escape into the calm at our house. Plus, since I don't have a dog of my own, I get to play with hers a lot. It works out for both of us.

Once we're all cooled off again, we get to have free play for the rest of P.E. Nadine, Emery, Tino, and I wander over to the trail that circles around the field. Tino and I step up on a tree trunk that has fallen over and balance as we walk across. Emery takes a stick and starts poking the dirt, stirring up a little dust cloud. Nadine crouches down and turns over a rock.

"Look! Look at all the bugs!" she calls. I hop down off the tree trunk and we crowd around to see a centipede, some ants, and two spiders scurry away. Three potato bugs curl into a ball.

"Cool!" says Emery. As he crouches down, a cricket jumps out from the tall grass and goes flying over his shoulder. "Whoa!" he says, falling to the ground. But within a second, he's back on his feet and trying to catch the cricket.

Tino is right behind him, but I get lucky and catch one that is jumping the other way. "Got it!" I shout, and we all start running over to Ping to show him what we found.

"Awesome, guys!" he says with a broad smile. "There are a lot of them out this time of year. You could say it's cricket season."

When Nadine comes over to see, I open my hands to show her. I try to crack my hands open so she can look in without the cricket escaping, but I open them too wide and it jumps straight out at her and lands on her head. She looks shocked and unsure whether to laugh or cry, but everyone else starts laughing and Ping gently scoops it out of her hair so she relaxes again.

Then Ping turns to the rest of the class and shouts, "Ten more minutes!"

We all run across the field for one more shot at the goal. Tino and Nadine score, but my ball hits the goalpost and bounces away. Emery's ball isn't even close. We run after the balls to collect them, drop them in the bag, and head in for lunch.

* * *

The cafeteria has broccoli cheese stuffed potatoes at lunch and it's Eat a Rainbow Day at the salad bar. Nadine is piling shredded carrots and dragon fruit on her salad. This is the first year we've had dragon fruit in the salad bar. It is white with little seeds in it that look like a poppy seed muffin. I grab a slice and take a little nibble. It kind of tastes like a kiwi, but not as sweet. We sit down next to Emery, who is already eating a peanut butter and jelly sandwich from home. He slides down on the bench to make room for us at the long table in the cafeteria.

Near the end of lunch, our principal walks in and announces that we will have special visitors from the high school today who will be performing a dance for us after lunch, so everyone is to stay seated when they have finished eating. A buzz fills the room as everyone starts talking at once. After a few minutes, the sound dies down and we pull our legs out from underneath the table, spin around on the bench, and sit backward at the table to face the stage.

When it's quiet, the curtains on the stage open. Several high school students are frozen like statues in various poses on the stage. One girl starts to beat a drum with a slow *bum, bum, bum* rhythm and one of the dancers starts to move to the beat. A tall boy jangles a bell, and another dancer unfreezes and dances with light fluttering movements. Every time a new instrument starts, another dancer moves in time with it, until the room is full of music and movement that blends together in the most marvelous way.

It's so beautiful! I let the melody and movement swim around in my head as we walk to social studies. Colby introduces our new topic. We will be studying cultures, what makes cultures unique, and how we can all learn from differences in each other's cultures.

We get out our special notebooks and Colby instructs us to write about a special occasion in our family and how we celebrate it. I think about it for a while and decide to write about how we celebrate birthdays. We actually celebrate two birthdays for me—the day that I was born as well as the day that I was adopted.

Daddy, Papa, and I each have a special birthday plate that we use every year on our birthdays. We went to Color Me Mine in Boulder to make them. Each plate has our handprint in the middle, "Happy Birthday" on the top around the rim, and our name at the bottom. They are beautiful. Papa is a really good artist and wrote the letters in paint from these little paint jars you can squeeze. Now, every year on our birthday, we take the plate out and eat a special dinner or treat on it. We always put a candle on top and sing "Happy Birthday."

For the birthday of the day I was born, I usually get to play with friends or have a party. And for my adoption birthday, I do something special with Daddy and Papa.

Both days are super fun, but they're different. The party with my friends is louder and all about doing fun things. At my family party, we read a scrapbook we've written about our life together as a family, and then we write another page about what has happened over the last year to add to it. We also write a letter to my birth mom and birth dad and pick out a photo of me to send to them.

Once I finish writing about my special occasion in my notebook, I have filled up two and a half pages. I pick up some colored pencils and start coloring a picture of myself on my birthday. I draw my birthday plate and a carrot muffin with a candle in it. Then I make thought bubbles like little clouds that drift from one page to the next and make a really big thought bubble to show what I am thinking. Or actually, what I am wishing for.

My wish is always the same—to get a dog. I draw a picture of a brown dog with curly hair wagging its tail. Or at least I try to show that the tail is wagging, but it's kind of hard to show that in a picture, so I write in little words next to it "wagging its tail" because it kind of looks like a blur. But it's okay, it looks like it's happy and that's the most important part. Just thinking about it makes me happy, so I color pretty hearts around the rest of the pages until the bell rings.

* * *

I drag my feet as we walk to the computer lab. My head feels heavy and I slump into my chair. We watch my computer teacher give a slideshow presentation that she made about her family vacation, and then we get to put our own slideshow together with clip art to show what we did with our own family over the summer. I look around and everyone else is already working, clicking away on their computers. I try to think and think, but my brain feels fuzzy. I lay my head down on the table.

I picture my family—Daddy, Papa, Artemis, and Orion. I also picture Nadine and Pia, their mom and dad, and, of course, their dogs. Sometimes we all get together over the holidays and then it really feels like a big family. I remember last year we all spent Thanksgiving together and the house was so warm and everyone was talking and laughing and playing games and it felt so full of love . . .

My head feels heavier, and my eyes close.

Everyone helped cook, but the turkey took forever . . . the music was playing *bum, bum, bum* . . . and then little bells started and the turkey started dancing . . . when Papa tried to take it out of the oven, it tried to fly away . . .

"Sophie, are you okay?" My computer teacher is looking down at me with concern. I was dreaming.

"I'm sorry, I must have fallen asleep," I mumble apologetically.

"Do you feel well?" she asks, touching my forehead with the back of her hand. "You're hot. Why don't you go to the nurse's office?"

"Okay, thank you," I say and drag myself out of my chair.

The nurse takes my temperature—101.5 degrees. I have a fever. He calls Papa and sends me back to the classroom to get my backpack. Then I wait in the office for Papa to get there. I sit on a chair, put my backpack on the table, and rest my face on my backpack. The walls blur together. I breathe in and breathe out, over and over.

When Papa gets me, he takes me straight home and puts me in bed. I slide under the covers with a shiver. "I'm freezing," I tell him and he piles more blankets on top of me. I feel him sit down at the bottom of my bed and rest his hand on my leg, and I feel another weight on my feet that must be Orion. Then everything is darkness.

* * *

When I wake up, it's dark outside and I hear low voices from downstairs. Daddy must be home. I see water and saltine crackers on the shelf next to my bed, so I take a drink then lie back down again. I don't feel hungry enough to eat anything.

The hallway light flickers on and Daddy peers into my bedroom. "Daddy," I manage to say, almost a whisper.

He walks in, reaches down, and feels my head. First my forehead, then my temple. "Let's take your temperature."

It's 102 degrees, so it's gone up. "My throat hurts," I moan.

He tells me to sit up while he gets some medicine. He comes back and squeezes some gooey liquid into a little plastic cup. It tastes like bubble gum, which I like better than the grape flavored medicine, but it's still not as good as real bubble gum. I swallow it as quickly as I can and then wash it down with water. I still don't want anything to eat. "Read me a story, Daddy."

He pulls out a book, settles himself down, and starts to read. He doesn't get very far before I can't keep my eyes open and the words blur together as I drift off to sleep.

* * *

Sometime in the middle of the night, I wake up. My stomach feels so bad and I'm hot and cold all at once. I try to get out of bed and realize I'm going to be sick. I try to run to the bathroom, but I am too late. I feel like I can't breathe, and I am crying. "Daddy! Papa!" I shout.

They both come running down the hall looking sleepy, but their faces are creased with worry. Papa helps me change my clothes and Daddy cleans everything up. They walk me back to my bed and Daddy hands me my water. I manage to take a sip and have one bite of a saltine cracker.

Then I snuggle up under the mountain of blankets with only my eyes poking out. My eyes are too heavy, and I quickly slide back down into deep, dark sleep.

* * *

In the morning, I wake to sunshine blazing through my room. It sparkles on the ceiling and dances across my stuffies, making polka dots across my stuffed dog's face. I squeeze him close to me, rubbing his soft fur on my cheek. I must have slept late.

When I feel good enough to get out of bed, I find Papa working in his office. He turns and smiles when he hears me come in. "How are you doing, sweet pea?"

"I'm hungry," I answer without thinking.

"Good, that's a good sign," he says.

We head downstairs and he fixes me a small bowl of oatmeal with bananas on top. It's not as big as I would normally eat, but I can't even finish half of it. "That's okay," he assures me as he scoops the leftovers into the compost. Normally, we would save our leftovers to eat later, but not when I'm sick.

I'm still really tired, so we spend the rest of the morning reading together on the couch. When I start to yawn, Papa puts on the *Tinker Bell* movie for me, but I fall asleep right away.

I wake up on the couch with a blanket tucked around me when I hear the door open. Daddy is home. He gives Papa a quick kiss, then comes in to check on me. I smile and hold his hand as he takes my temperature. "Only 99.2, almost back to normal," he says encouragingly.

I realize I'm hungry again, so Papa puts together a bowl of broth with a few noodles. It's the best when I'm not feeling well. It makes me feel like it is working some healing magic from the inside out.

* * *

The next day, I feel so much better. I rush into Daddy and Papa's room first thing in the morning to ask if I can go back to school. Papa laughs and says, "That's a good sign, and you look great, but because you had a fever yesterday, you have to stay home today."

I finally feel hungry—no, actually, I feel famished!

Papa makes sweet potato and egg scramble and slices up fruit on the side, and I hungrily gobble it up and ask for more. He gives me a little bit more and tells me to go slow.

But I don't want to go slow. I feel great. "Let's go for a walk!" I suggest happily and zip down the hall to brush my teeth, throw on my jacket, and put on my shoes.

"Hang on, hang on," Papa mumbles slowly as he dillydallies around in the kitchen.

"May I wait outside?" I ask. Then I remember that I was supposed to get together with Nadine after school the day I got sick. "And may I go down to Nadine's house before she goes to school? She invited me over to play before I got sick. Maybe I can play with her this afternoon instead? Please?"

"Sure, but don't go inside their house. Just let them know that you're better and see if they're free this afternoon."

Daddy gives me a quick hug and kiss as he heads off to work, and tells me to take it easy, if not for my sake, then for Papa's. I don't know why they're so tired. I was the one who was sick and I feel great now, but I say I will anyway.

When I get to Nadine's house, she answers the door with one shoe on. "Sophie!" she says and a smile bursts across her face. "Hang on, I have something for you."

I stand on the front step while Nadine spins around and dashes up the stairs. The door is open a crack and I hear her little sister, Pia, screaming and the dogs barking.

Nadine opens the door all the way again and hands me

a card. A rainbow with at least ten different colors arches across the top of the page, and written across the top of that are the words "get well soon." Underneath the rainbow, she drew a picture of us together next to all three of her dogs.

"It's beautiful. Thank you," I tell her, giving her a huge smile. "Can you play at the creek after school today? I'm all better, I just have to wait until tomorrow to go back to school."

"Yeah, that sounds fun," Nadine says, tying her other shoe. "I gotta go, but I'll see you after school."

Seeing Nadine makes me feel even better than I was already feeling, and I skip back to my house holding the card, a smile spreading across my face.

Chapter 4

When Nadine gets home from school, she comes straight over to my house. I hear the knock at the front door and race to answer it. She gives me a big squeeze and we start talking a mile a minute and laughing.

Nadine's dad, Marcelo, agrees to take us down to the creek so Papa can rest, so I shout goodbye and pull on my jacket and shoes. "Don't forget your sunglasses and sunhat! And have fun, I love you!" Papa hollers down the hall.

Outside, we dash over to Nadine's house where Marcelo is zipping up Pia's jacket and the dogs are prancing around excitedly in a circle.

"May we walk them, please?" I ask as soon as we get close enough for him to hear over the barking.

"Yes, Sophie, that would be great. Why don't you take Luna, and Nadine can take Ginger? I've got Patch since he's probably too big for you."

We grab the leashes and the dogs practically pull us down the sidewalk and onto the trail. Pretty soon we are running, smiling, and laughing. It feels like I was never sick at all. When we reach the dog park where we can take their leashes off, the dogs charge full steam ahead into the water, jumping and splashing and barking with joy. Nadine and I laugh as we watch Ginger, the light brown Lab, try to take a running leap across the creek and land with a splash in the middle. As she tries to shake off, Luna races toward her, dodging to the side at the last minute to avoid crashing right into her.

"They are so silly," I tell Nadine, then add, "you are so lucky."

She nods her head and then says, "It's so good to see you again."

* * *

Halloween is coming up soon and I don't know what I'm going to be yet. Last year I was a cat, and the year before that I was a dragon. We always look for a great dog costume, but we've never been able to find one. I hope that we'll find one this year, but when Daddy takes me out shopping, we don't find anything. There's a giraffe, a monster, and lots of monkey costumes. The only dog costume we find is a plain brown pair of pants and shirt with some flimsy dog ears that don't really stay attached to the headband. There's not even a tail or anything.

That night, I ask Papa if he can make me a dog costume. Papa is an artist, but he doesn't usually sew. He thinks it over and agrees to give it a try. We sketch out an idea of what I want it to look like. I tell him that I want it to be light brown with a dark brown spot on the belly, and the sweetest little ears sticking out of the top. He draws the face and ears on a hood that I can pull snugly over my head. I tell him I want it to have the softest fur. Papa nods and says he'll even make a perfectly sized tail too. I jump up and clap my hands. I can't wait!

* * *

By the time Halloween comes around, most of the trees have lost their leaves, and a chilly wind freezes me down to my bones.

Papa has finished my costume, and it is amazing! I pull the hood snug over my head and prance into school, trotting happily like a dog. It's fun to see everyone walking in to school all dressed up. There is a robot made out of a cardboard box, and so many animals hopping and prancing and meowing, and even a rainbow with little clouds hanging down on each side.

I look around for Nadine and finally see her when I get to the classroom. She is dressed up like a baby, with little pigtails off to each side and pajamas that go all the way down to her ankles. Her feet are stuffed into white bunny rabbit slippers and she is sucking on a pacifier.

She pulls the pacifier out of her mouth and asks, "What do you think? Daddy let me use one of Pia's old binkies, just for today."

"You look so cozy! What does the binky taste like?" I ask curiously.

She takes it out of her mouth and lets it fall onto the ribbon tied around her neck so it swings back and forth across her chest as she talks. "It doesn't taste like much actually. It was really fun at first, but I didn't realize how hard it is to eat or do anything with it. I have to take it out of my mouth every time I talk."

Just then, the robot walks in and waddles over to us. There is a big cardboard box where its arms stick out and a smaller cardboard box over its head. Big, green deely boppers made out of pipe cleaners stick out of its head. A rectangular robot mouth is drawn on the face, and two holes for the eyes are cut into the box.

Once I look inside and see the face, I realize it's Emery. "Whoa! Cool costume," I say, admiring it.

"Thanks," he says and tries to turn around, tilting to one side and catching himself. "Moving in it is kind of hard, though."

It's hard to concentrate because everyone is so full of excitement. When Maddie and Magnolia walk in, both dressed as bumble bees, everyone rushes over to pet Maddie and squeal in delight. Then, as always happens with Maddie, everyone calms down and settles in to learn the math lesson. Even with Maddie's little bumble bee wings sticking up, she is as calm as ever and somehow relaxes us and helps us focus.

During library time, Aldo reads *Thank You, Mr. Falker*, a story about a girl who mixes up words in her head and has a hard time learning to read.

At writing time, we are asked to write about a time when we had to face a challenge and how we overcame it. I think about it for a long time. I think about how Mr. Falker helped the girl in that story understand that her brain worked differently in order to learn to read.

I don't know what to write about. I have two daddies who love me, and two of the sweetest cats who cuddle up on my feet at night. Nadine lives down the street and I've made so many friends at school. But sometimes waiting to get a dog is a challenge for me.

I start writing about how hard it is to be patient all the time. And how I don't understand when Daddy says we don't have time for a dog because he works too much. But how I try to do my chores anyway and show him that I'll take care of it. I've been asking for a dog for years and sometimes I feel like it will never happen.

I look over at Nadine and she has written two pages already. "What are you writing about?" I ask her.

She blushes a little bit, then says, "About having a little sister. Like, how at first it was pretty easy, but now that she's talking so much and my parents are so busy, it's hard." Shrugging, she says, "I don't know. I love her a lot and I'm really glad we got a baby, but . . ." and trails off.

"I know," I say. "You miss having your parents just to yourself."

"Yeah, sometimes I wish it could just be us again, even for a little bit," she says and looks down.

I nod, wondering what it would be like to have a little brother or sister. "What are you writing about overcoming it?" I ask.

Nadine looks up and smiles. "I was writing about how much you've helped me. Because you're still there to play with, and you make me laugh, and you always understand me when you listen."

We grin at each other and get up to hand in our papers. Emery comes over and tries to put his big robot arms around us, but he is too blocky and nearly tips over, and we all dissolve into a fit of laughter.

It's finally time for the parade around the school. Everyone gets ready and lines up. When we walk out of the classroom, the hallway is crowded with people. Parents and grandparents line the halls, and kids in every grade are tromping, dancing, hopping, or twirling down the hall in their costumes. I wave as we pass by Papa. Daddy couldn't come because he had to work.

* * *

That evening after school, we go trick-or-treating. I pretend to be a puppy and say, "Arf! Arf!" the whole way. That makes Daddy and Papa laugh. When we get home, I ask again if we can get a puppy. Daddy sighs and Papa looks down.

"Sweetheart, a dog is a big responsibility," Daddy explains. "And we need a lot of time to take care of it. As it is, we barely have enough time to take care of the cats."

"Why don't we get more time?" I ask reasonably. I'm not seeing what the problem is.

"Well, I'm working on a big project at work and there's a bug in it that we just can't find," he explains.

I stare at him for a minute and then ask, "A bug? I know what bugs look like. I could help you find it."

Daddy laughs and says, "Not that kind of bug. I mean a problem with the instructions for the computer program we're building."

"Oh."

"And because this bug is causing so many problems, we're getting way behind and have to work a lot to figure it all out," Daddy continues. "I don't even have as much time to spend with you as I want."

I'm still not giving up. "Yeah, but you could come home earlier. Or not stay late as much. And Papa doesn't work that much." That's mostly true. Sometimes he doesn't work much at all and other times we barely see him because he is working all the time. I know what they're going to say before they even say it.

When they tell me again that we can't get a dog right now, my face falls and I feel like I'm about to start crying. "But I'll be the one to take care of it, so you guys won't even need more time. I'll walk the dog and feed it and play with it and everything," I beg. Now I really am crying.

"Come on, sweet pea," Papa says and scoops me into his arms and carries me up the stairs. "It has been a long day and a late night, and we need to get you to bed." I bury my head into his shoulder and start sobbing. It's not fair! I want a dog more than anything in the world. And it would be great, I just know it would.

* * *

I still feel sad when I go downstairs for breakfast in the morning. Papa notices and tries to tickle me playfully, but I'm not in the mood. It was so amazing dressing up like a dog for Halloween, but now I feel like all I'll ever be able to do is pretend. Pretend to be a dog, or pretend that we could ever get a dog. It doesn't matter.

"Sophie, Daddy and I talked last night, and we know you're really sad about not having a dog."

I look up curiously.

"While our answer is still no . . ."

I look down again quickly, and glumly stare into my bowl of oatmeal.

". . . we want you to understand that even though we don't have the time or energy to bring a dog into the family right now, we are working on it." He takes a deep breath. "You know, it's actually something that we've been realizing for a while now—that Daddy and I have taken on too much at work and need to cut back. I know things have gotten kind of crazy and we haven't been there as much, so we want you to know that we're going to try to make changes. It won't happen overnight, but hopefully it will soon."

That makes me look up eagerly. "How soon? Okay, I know not, like, tomorrow, but maybe next week?" I ask, suddenly hopeful once again.

He chuckles. "No darling, it could be a few months or a year or more. It depends on a lot of things falling into place."

I don't know what that means. I mean, if they want to change something, why not just change it? Why wait? There are some things I don't understand about grown-ups at all. But who knows, maybe we won't have to wait as long as Papa says. You never know.

Chapter 5

The next day is Saturday, so when I wake up, I stay in my pajamas and pick out a book to read in bed while I wait for my parents to wake up. I choose *Buddy* from The Puppy Place series. I've read a lot of these books, and each time I hope that Lizzie and Charles will be able to keep the dog they're fostering. After I read a few chapters, I put down the book and start drawing pictures of puppies all over my notebook.

After a while, Daddy wakes up and pops his head in my door. "Good morning, sunshine. You're going to have a whole herd of dogs in that notebook before long."

"Hi, Daddy. It's not a herd; it's a pack or a litter. Do you like this one? I gave him spots," I respond.

He bends down to see my notebook. "It's really good," he says. "I like the one with the bow on its head."

Nadine's birthday party is today. After breakfast, I make a birthday card and go upstairs to pick out a present. I go into Papa's office and pull a big cardboard box off the bookshelf. I kneel down on the floor and sort through the art materials inside. Because Papa is an artist, he is always getting free samples of new art supplies or extra boxes of fancy markers and paints. The ones that he doesn't use, he puts in a box for me to use or to give as gifts.

I know Nadine really likes coloring, so I find an activity book and a box of colored pencils. The colored pencils are fancy and sharpened to a fine point, just waiting to create something beautiful.

"Ooh, those look nice," Papa says as he walks in. "Want help wrapping them?"

I shake my head. "No, I've got it."

I pull a wicker basket full of pretty cloth material off the shelf and dig through it until I find a soft velvety cloth just the right size. I lay the cloth down on the ground and set the activity book and pencils on top, then fold the edges over and wrap it all together. Finally, I take a glass jar full of ribbons off the shelf and pick out a pretty green ribbon with purple polka dots. I tie the bow around the present and set it aside.

When I'm done, I make a friendship bracelet with red and blue beads on the ends and a big bead with the letter N on it in the middle. Then I tie it to the ribbon.

I go downstairs and find Daddy getting home from a run. "May we go to the park, Daddy? Please?"

"Sorry, Sophie, I've got to shower and get to work. Plus, you need to do your chores before Nadine's party. Is your room clean yet?"

I am about to say "yes" when I hear Papa call down from upstairs, "Sophie! Please come put away the art stuff you took out!"

Daddy nods and I trudge back upstairs.

I quickly scoop up the cloth and ribbons and shove everything back on the bookshelf, then shout, "I'm done!"

Papa looks in and says, "Good, now please get your dirty clothes and clean your room."

I pull my laundry basket out of my closet and set it in

the middle of my room, then pick up a pair of jeans off the floor and toss it toward the basket. I haul a pile of shirts out from under my bed and aim them one by one at the basket. Each time I make a basket, I imagine myself as a basketball star and give myself two points.

I carry my laundry basket downstairs and watch as Papa pulls my clothes right-side out and sorts them into piles. Our laundry room is filled with mountains of every different color. Papa says if you wash the reds with the whites, everything will turn out pink. He helps me measure the laundry detergent, then I add the soap and he adds the clothes. I get to push the buttons and hear the washing machine whir to a start.

Next I head to my room to pick up my toys and books. I try to be responsible so I can get a dog. I do a good job at first, but then I get distracted and start reading *Buddy* again. I'm surprised when Papa sticks his head in the door and says it's time to go to the party already.

Nadine is having her birthday party at the Butterfly Pavilion, a zoo for insects. When I get there, I set her present down on the table in a back room and then join everyone climbing and running in the play area.

"Sophie! You're here!" Nadine shouts.

She's smiling and climbing across a play structure shaped like a large, purple centipede. I run over and climb across a rope spider web. After a few minutes, Nadine's dad hollers that it's time to get started, so we all scramble down and get in line for the butterfly room.

"Welcome to the Butterfly Pavilion!" a short man with

brown hair greets us. He holds a door open and we squish into a tiny room facing another set of doors. The first door has to be all the way closed before we can open the next door, to make sure no butterflies get out.

"The oil on your skin is very harmful to the butterflies," he tells us. "So it's important not to let a butterfly land on you, because that will shorten its life. If one does land on you, please hold still and wait for it to fly off on its own. Don't try to pick it up."

We nod and he opens the second door. As we step in, I feel like we're in a jungle. The air is warm and heavy mist floats down from the ceiling. The room is so big I can't see the walls or the end of the path, and plants are everywhere I look. Big plants with dark green leaves. Short plants with bright pink flowers. And butterflies flying every which way around the plants. There are so many butterflies it's hard to keep track of them all. Big blue ones, orange and black ones, and small white ones flit from leaf to leaf. We walk down the twisty trails between the plants.

"Look!" Nadine says, pointing to a bright green leaf next to the trail.

We lean over to see four tiny, white eggs on a nice green leaf, just like in the book *A Very Hungry Caterpillar*. "Wow," we murmur, crowding in to see it.

"I can't believe the eggs don't roll off the leaf," Emery says.

When we stand up, our hair is sparkling with dew from the mist falling gently down. I look over at Nadine. Her wet hair is plastered to her forehead, and she is beaming. I can tell she's having the best birthday ever.

We cram back into the little room between doors. The brown-haired man checks everyone for butterflies. Once he has determined that there are no butterflies clinging to our clothes or hair, he lets us open the door back into the main building.

Next we look at some of the other insects and quickly get in line to see Rosie the spider. Rosie is kind of famous and everyone loves her.

"Rosie is a Chilean rose-hair tarantula," the lady holding Rosie explains.

We all lean closer to watch Rosie gracefully lift her thick, fuzzy legs and walk along the lady's hand. Rosie is a really big spider—about the size of my fist.

"She is perfectly safe for you to hold, but please remember that you are much, much bigger than she is so be careful not to drop her," the lady continues. "Many tarantulas around the world are endangered, and we're trying to bring their population back up."

Nadine gets to go first since she's the birthday girl. The lady takes Nadine's outstretched hand and gently places Rosie onto it.

Nadine smiles and her face lights up even brighter than before. Nadine's dad, Marcelo, snaps a photo of her and then Nadine gently hands Rosie back to the lady, who gives her a sticker that says, "I held Rosie!"

The lady then passes Rosie to the rest of us in line one by one. When she comes to Marcelo, she asks if he'd like to hold Rosie.

"Nope, no thank you," he says and quickly takes a few steps back.

Nadine's mom, Cordelia, bravely places her hand out and holds Rosie for a second. "Oh, she's not as scary as I thought. You can barely feel her. You sure you don't want to try, Marcelo?" she asks, but Marcelo has already moved to the other side of the room and is looking at something in a glass case.

Cordelia hands Rosie back and proudly puts her "I held Rosie!" sticker on her jacket.

I stick out my hand with my palm facing up and wait for the gentle touch of Rosie stepping onto my hand. Her touch is light and delicate, as though Rosie were a ballerina dancer. I know some people are afraid of spiders, but Rosie isn't scary at all. I lean in close and whisper to her, "I'm sorry your family is going extinct. I'll do everything I can to help you stay alive."

After I put on my "I held Rosie!" sticker, it's time for a birthday snack and presents. We line up to wash our hands and sit down at a long table in the back room, grateful for a cool glass of water. Everyone has a zucchini bread muffin on a napkin in front of them, and Nadine's muffin has nine candles on top. We sing "Happy Birthday" and her dad slides her presents across the table to her.

Nadine chooses my present to open first and squeals. With a quick "thanks," she reaches for another one. This one is a beautiful paint set, filled with the most vivid colors imaginable. It looks super grown-up, and I know that

Nadine will love it. She thanks Tino and sets it aside next to my opened present.

As Nadine pauses to take a bite of her muffin, everyone hears a *crash!* and whirls around to see Pia sitting on the floor next to the paint set. The case is shattered and some of the paints have fallen out and broken on the floor. There's no way Nadine can put it back together.

"Pia!" Nadine growls, and Pia's eyes start to fill up with tears.

Nadine's dad scoops Pia up, and her mom bends down to clean up the paints. Now the bright smile that has been on Nadine's face all day is gone. A big storm cloud has settled over it instead and her lower lip quivers.

"She didn't mean to, sweetheart," Nadine's mom tells her gently.

"I don't care! She is always ruining my stuff, and it's not fair!" Nadine is fighting to not break down in tears in the middle of her birthday party.

"I know, sweet pea, I know," her mom says and rubs her back. "I'm sorry. Those looked like really incredible paints too. You were really looking forward to using those."

Nadine nods and takes a deep breath, but a frown remains on her face. "It's no fun having a little sister," she pouts.

"Here, you can open my present next," Emery says. Then he adds through a mouthful of muffin, "It's not even breakable."

Nadine shrugs, then laughs and unwraps the present.

Inside is a small, brown teddy bear. "Oh, he's so soft," Nadine coos, wrapping her arms around it. She holds onto it, squeezing tightly, and takes another deep breath.

After a minute, Pia comes over to Nadine with big, sorrowful eyes and tugs on her sleeve. Nadine turns and Pia leans into her for a hug.

Pia reaches up and tries to hand Nadine a little piece of the broken paints. Nadine takes it and right away I can see her heart getting softer again. Pia tugs on Nadine's sleeve and her lower lip begins to tremble.

Nadine takes a big breath, then sighs and says, "It's okay, Pia. Want to sit on my lap?"

Pia nods and climbs up onto Nadine's lap. Nadine hands her the polka dot ribbon from my present, and Pia tightly clutches it in her chubby hands.

Since I'm sitting the closest to Nadine, I am the only one who hears her when she leans over and whispers into Pia's ear, "I'm sorry I got mad at you, Pia. I'm glad you're here. When we get home, you can color with my new colored pencils with me."

* * *

The next week at school, everyone gets to choose an animal and its habitat to do our mid-year report on. Of course, my favorite animals are dogs, but since we're focusing on wild animals, I decide to do my report on Arctic foxes. At first, I wasn't sure if a fox is more like a dog or a cat since I've never really seen one, but Colby says they are closer to dogs so I decide that it's perfect.

Our first step is to do some research so we can make a habitat book and write about what we've learned. I pick out a book about Arctic foxes and start reading. I learn that because they live in the Arctic, they have adaptations that help them survive in really cold places. An adaptation is how an animal has changed to better survive in the place where it lives. So Arctic foxes have really thick fur to keep them warm in the cold snow where they live. They also have short, round bodies to keep their heat inside.

But the coolest thing I read is that their fur actually changes color throughout the year! In the winter, they have beautiful, white fur that helps them blend into the white of the snow all around them. When they blend in, it's harder for other animals who might want to eat them to see them. Then, in the summer, their fur changes to a pretty shade of brown to blend in with the ground. I can't imagine changing color twice a year. What colors would I be?

As I read, I also learn that Arctic foxes are having a harder time finding food because of climate change. Colby says that our climate is getting warmer because there is so much carbon dioxide in the air. As the temperature rises, the sea ice where the foxes hunt melts. Colby tells us that there are things we can do to help. As he tells us about using better lightbulbs and driving less, I picture the Arctic foxes and decide that I will do everything I can to keep them safe so they have food to eat.

I start writing down facts into my habitat book and before I know it, the bell rings and I have to turn in my book.

* * *

In social studies, Colby tells us to write about a time when we experienced a different culture. He adds, "Make sure to describe what went well, what you liked, what you didn't like, how it made you feel, and if you would do it again."

I have to think about this for a while. Most of my life has been spent in only one culture—here in Lafayette, Colorado with Daddy and Papa. But last year, we also spent a few weeks with Daddy's family in Seattle. Daddy's sister works downtown and we walked all around Seattle with her.

That was a much different culture because it was such a big city. Taxi cabs zoomed by and city buses thundered down the clogged streets. I held tightly onto Daddy's hand while we crossed the street. People filled the sidewalks and the skyscrapers disappeared into the clouds.

I liked watching the fish throwers toss big, slimy fish to each other at Pike Place Market. Eventually though, after all of that walking, I got tired and my legs felt like rubber walking up and down the hills. Daddy said I was getting hangry, which is when I get angry because I'm hungry, so we stopped and ate sushi for lunch. Even though some parts of the trip were hard, I would do it again.

I lean over toward Nadine and whisper, "What are you writing about?"

"Remember when we went to Japan a few years ago? It was spring and the cherry blossoms smelled so good. I didn't really understand what people were saying because the language is so different, but the soba noodles and miso soup were the best! And the plane ride was so long I slept like an entire night and was still flying in the air when I woke up!"

We hand our papers in and listen to everyone else talk about the different cultures they've experienced. Colby shows us pictures of different places he's lived around the world. In one photo, he is smiling in the bright sun in Mexico. In another, he's standing on a bridge in the wind in England, his hair blown across his face. He is smiling in every photo and his eyes light up as he shares them with us. Someday when I grow up, I hope I can travel to a different country too.

Chapter 6

The weather is colder, geese are flying overhead, and Thanksgiving is here. We are having Nadine's family, Nana and Gramps, my aunt and uncle, and my cousins over to our house this year. It's one of my favorite times of the year because our home gets so loud and warm and crazy. And smells so delicious.

When I wake up on Thanksgiving morning, it is only me and Daddy and Papa, and the house is still and quiet. I stretch my legs all the way down to my toes, and Artemis jumps off my bed to find a calmer place to sleep.

The sun is shining through my bedroom window as I reach over to my bookshelf to grab a book to read. *Ava and Taco Cat.* I love how Ava enjoys the way words are spelled, especially palindromes that are spelled the same way forward and backward. Of course, I totally understand how she feels about wanting a pet so bad.

Reading the book reminds me of how lucky I am to have two amazing cats. I can't imagine not having any pets at all. Usually either Artemis or Orion sleeps on my bed at night, and I love listening to their rumbling purrs when I scratch under their chins or stroke their heads gently. They make me laugh so much, like the time we put out birdseed in our backyard and a squirrel came over to eat it. Suddenly, Artemis got real quiet and hunched down in front of the sliding glass door, then starting making little chirping noises, her whole body low on the ground, crouching, ready to pounce. Or the time Orion helped us unpack our Christmas decorations, jumping and pouncing on all of the ribbons and strings of lights. Just thinking about them reminds me that they are such a great part of our family.

Pretty soon, I hear Daddy and Papa downstairs, clanking dishes, running water, and laughing. I smile and keep reading. By the time I finish the chapter and put the book down, I realize I am starving. I lope downstairs and the kitchen is already exploding in color and sound. Jazz music is playing while Papa chops carrots into tiny pieces to add to the mound of celery, onions, and bread crumbs for the stuffing. Daddy smiles when he sees me and hands me a plate of steaming hot dumplings.

"Yum!" I say, smiling and taking a seat at the table where I can watch what they're doing at the counter. Hot vegetable dumplings are the best Thanksgiving morning breakfast ever. Everything always smells so good when we're cooking a Thanksgiving meal, and Daddy understands that I can't wait all day to eat all of that delicious food.

I even eat seconds while I watch Daddy stuff the turkey. Then in one monstrous effort, they put the turkey into the oven and set the timer. Daddy starts to clean up the kitchen while Papa helps me make the cranberry sauce.

I get out the bag of cranberries from the fridge, dump them into the colander, and rinse them off. Then I wash an orange and peel off the little sticker. Papa lets me use his sharp knife to cut the orange in half, then half again. Next

I plop the orange slices in the blender and add the rest of the cranberries on top. My favorite part is adding a little bit of honey. I try not to get it everywhere, but somehow my shirt ends up sticky anyway.

Papa closes the lid of the blender and says, "Go ahead!"

I hit the button and quickly put my hands over my ears while the blender churns everything smooth like applesauce. Every now and then, Papa stops the blender, sticks a spoon in and stirs it, pushing the mixture on the sides down so the blender can catch everything that gets stuck. After a few more whirls, it's all blended. I pour it into a little dish, Papa clicks the lid into place, and I put it in the fridge for later. Then we all sit down at the kitchen table and play Chutes and Ladders while we wait for everyone to get to our house.

* * *

Nana and Gramps are the first to arrive. I run to the door as soon as I hear the knock and burst into Nana's arms when the door opens.

"Sophie!" Nana says, squeezing me tightly.

"Happy Thanksgiving!" Gramps says cheerfully, leaning over my head to hand Daddy a heavy casserole dish. Then he bends down and tickles me, and plants a quick kiss on my cheek.

Minutes later, the rest of the family tumbles in—Uncle Leopold and Aunt Vina with my cousins Bianca and Orlando. They are followed shortly by Nadine and her family. This is when the fun really gets going. I am practically jumping in the air for joy with so much excitement, and all of us kids are running around the house squealing while Uncle Leopold chases us, pretending that he will gobble us up.

"Okay then, I think it's time for our turkey trot!" Daddy shouts. "Everyone who wants to run around Waneka Lake, come with me. And everyone who wants a decent chance at a sense of sanity and quiet before the wild animals return, please make yourselves at home."

Daddy, Papa, and Uncle Leopold wrangle all of us out of the house and everyone grabs a bike.

A minute later, Nadine's mom, Cordelia, rushes out of the house and says, "Wait for me! I'm coming too!"

Pia and Bianca sit in the buggy hooked up to Cordelia's bike since they're too small to bike on their own. Daddy and Papa jog beside us as we pedal along the trail and head toward the lake. The sky is bright blue and the lake is calm. Ice has formed halfway across the lake, and hundreds of geese are standing, sitting, or walking on the ice. I hear their loud honks all the way from the shore.

We pull over next to the bike racks, and Nadine, Orlando, and I hop off as quickly as we can. We don't wait for Uncle Leopold to unhook Pia and Bianca from the buggy before racing over to the playground. When I reach the top of the slide, I turn and see Daddy salute Uncle Leopold and continue jogging with Papa and Cordelia all the way around the lake.

* * *

A couple of hours later, everyone strolls back home, a little slower and calmer than before. When we open the door, the smell of roasting turkey greets us and reminds me how hungry I am again. With all the good smells and running around, no wonder I love to eat on Thanksgiving. Gramps is ready for us, and has already set out sandwiches and salads on the table. We wash up and grab a plate, then everyone sits down to eat.

After lunch, I invite Nadine, Pia, and my cousins into my room to play games. I give Pia and my little cousin, Bianca, some blocks that I used to play with when I was little. Then Nadine and I set up Go Fish to play with my older cousin, Orlando. After a while, Pia and Bianca start trying to take our cards, so we switch to Hoot Owl Hoot. Bianca listens to us as we explain how to play, but Pia doesn't want to follow the rules. Every time she draws a sun card, she sticks it back in the deck until she draws a color card.

Nadine starts to get upset, saying, "Pia, you have to play the first card you draw!"

But I don't mind mixing up the rules a little bit because we're just having fun together anyway. Before we can sort it out, though, Cordelia and Uncle Leopold come in to collect Pia and Bianca for naptime. After they leave, we go back to playing Go Fish until we're bored. Then we lie around in my room, chatting.

Nadine tells us that this year, she wants to learn how to ice skate. "I'm hoping that I'll get a pair of ice skates for

Christmas so I can practice a lot."

Orlando is a year younger than us and a little quieter. He says he doesn't want to ice skate; he wants to stay inside where it's warm and read.

"What do you like to read, Orlando?" I ask.

"I don't know, the *Never Girls*. And *Humphrey*. And Puppy Place," he says with a shrug.

My eyes light up. I love all of those books, but especially The Puppy Place series. I pull a few books off my bookshelf and hand them to him. "You can borrow these if you want. I wish we could foster a dog like Lizzie and Charles, but Daddy says we don't have time for one while he's working so much. Papa says they're going to try to not work as much so we can get a dog. I don't know why it has to take so long."

Nadine chimes in, "I know what you mean! Like, why can't I just get ice skates right now so I can start practicing and be really good by the time Christmas is here?"

Before we know it, Nana comes in my room with a bowlful of cucumber and jicama slices. "Are you hungry?" she asks. "You're welcome to eat in here, or you can come downstairs for one of Gramps's stories."

We scramble downstairs because we don't want to miss out on Gramps's story time. He has written a lot of books, and he is always working on something. When he's almost done with a story, he'll bring it over and read it to us. He calls us his little guinea pigs, though I don't see what that has to do with listening to his stories.

Anyway, today we all sit in a wide circle around him

on the living room floor and listen to his newest story about a little girl who has wings and can fly. But that's not the most interesting thing about her. The best thing about her is that she is really good at science, so when her class goes on a field trip to the planetarium and gets sucked into a black hole, she knows how to get them out safely.

I lean back on the couch and close my eyes as I listen. Whenever Gramps talks, I feel like I follow him all the way into the story until I am actually in another world. And I love the worlds he creates. Even Papa and Daddy take a break from cooking in the kitchen to sit down on a chair and listen as they sip hot spiced cider. I am so happy and cozy that I could fall asleep right here, and I almost do except that Gramps's story is too intriguing.

When he's done, he asks everyone what our favorite part was, and why, and if there was anything we didn't like. He listens to everyone, even the adults, but when he listens to us kids, I can tell he's listening the hardest. He says he likes to see the story through our eyes.

I tell him, "My favorite part was how she was good at science and knew how to use it to help her class."

As we talk, he jots down notes on his paper and his handwriting curls all the way around the page in fancy circles.

* * *

Finally, Pia and Bianca are up from their naps and dinner is almost ready.

I look out the window and shout, "It's snowing!

Look!"

Everyone gathers around and watches as the first snowflakes start to swirl down to the ground. The sun has disappeared and the sky is dense with gray clouds stuffed with snow.

The first snowfall of the year is always my favorite. It's magical and fills me with the most beautiful feeling of excitement and joy. Like anything is possible. All of a sudden, a thought pops into my head. It's actually more of a feeling than a thought. I feel, with certainty, that we are going to get a dog sooner than Daddy or Papa think. I don't say anything about it because some things just sound better when they're kept inside my head. Or my heart. I let it flutter down into this warm space in my heart, where it sits there happily waiting. And I am happy too, because I know I won't have to wait much longer.

Instead, I say, "May we go outside, Daddy? Please?"

Everyone agrees to take a short walk before dinner, and by the time we're bundled up and outside, there are hundreds of snowflakes swirling around. We stop at Nadine's house to grab her dogs, and now they're prancing around, hopping on their back legs, trying to catch the tiny snowflakes in their mouths.

It's much colder out now than it was this morning. My breath turns into a white puff of air that rises in front of me into a little cloud. The snow is the beautiful, fluffy kind that floats softly down to the ground. We walk along the creek path, the adults meandering along while we skip joyfully beside, and the snow keeps coming, thicker than the inside of a snow globe.

As the sun sets, the light fades into a deep shade of gray, turning the crisp air even colder. A shiver runs down my spine and I realize my legs and arms are numb. We turn back home, and when our door opens, the smell of turkey and the warmth of our home pull me inside. I shiver as I tug off my jacket, but I am smiling.

I hear Papa turn music on as I wash my hands and we all sit down at the table. Daddy serves up the steaming hot turkey, piles of sweet potatoes and green bean casserole, and the cranberry sauce Papa and I made. Before we eat, we all take turns telling what we're thankful for. Daddy is thankful for the run around the lake this morning, Papa is thankful for the music, Nana is thankful for her family and friends . . . around we go until it is my turn.

I know I might not have everything I want, but there is so much to be thankful for. I am thankful for Artemis and Orion. I am thankful for our house being so full and lively today. I am thankful for listening to Gramps's story. I am thankful for the yummy food. But what I say is that I am thankful for the snow, the first snowfall of the year. What I don't say is the feeling I still have, growing inside my heart, that knows with a fierce certainty that a dog is coming to us soon. I decide to keep that thought to myself for just a while longer.

* * *

That night after everyone has left, our house is calm and quiet again. It is late when Daddy and Papa tuck me in. I am so tired that I can barely keep my eyes open. But I still have enough energy to ask when we are volunteering and what we're going to do this year. It has been a tradition in our family to do some kind of volunteering over Thanksgiving weekend, and it usually ends up being the day after Thanksgiving.

Papa's whole face lights up into a smile. He and Daddy exchange a happy glance before he answers. "That is a great question, Sophie. Daddy and I decided that we should do something with dogs for our volunteering day this year."

My eyes open all the way and I try to sit up, but he shushes me back down.

"Tomorrow we'll go to the local shelter to help take care of the dogs they have there. We thought it would be a great way for you to see what you need to do to take care of a dog. And there are a lot of dogs out there that need a lot of love."

I am so excited, I can't believe it! "It's perfect!" I tell them, and reach around Papa's neck to give him the biggest hug ever. I sink back into my pillow and quickly fall asleep.

Chapter 7

The next day, I wake up slowly. Memories of Thanksgiving Day still swirl around in my head, and I lie in my bed for a while thinking of it all, wishing it could last forever. Then my eyes open with a start. We are volunteering at the animal shelter today! I jump out of bed and race down the hall. Daddy and Papa are still in bed.

I tumble excitedly into the middle and squeal, "I am sooo excited! Are you awake? When are we going?"

Papa smiles and mumbles something with his eyes closed that I can't understand.

Daddy leans over to give me a kiss on my cheek, yawns, and then asks, "Can you please share some of that energy with me? It's really not fair to keep it all to yourself." Then he sits up, adding, "We should get up; we're supposed to be there at nine."

* * *

The animal shelter is already busy by the time we arrive. Other families with kids, parents with older children, and groups of teenagers and college kids stand around chatting. Then Jazmin, a woman with a wide, friendly smile and curly, brown hair that bounces as she walks, comes in and divides us up into teams.

"We have a lot of animals here, and all of our little friends need lots of love, so please form yourselves into groups—dogs over here, cats over there, and all of the other smaller friends like rabbits and guinea pigs and hamsters over there," she instructs, pointing to different sides of the room.

We join the dog group, of course, which is led by Jazmin. She leads us around the corner and down the hallway so quickly that I almost have to run to keep up. Posters with pictures of dogs hang on the walls and say things like "A Dog is a Human's Best Friend" and "Dogs Leave Paw Prints on Your Heart."

Up ahead, Jazmin is saying, "We don't keep the animals in cages here like some other shelters do, because we've found that they tend to be happier and stay in better health when they have a chance to run around and play with each other."

I hurry to catch up and join the rest of the group as she leads us through a doorway and into the most amazing room filled with all kinds of dogs.

I walk inside and am swept into a swirling mass of excitement, love, and drool. A little white dog prances excitedly in a circle, yipping a song of welcome. I bend down and pet its soft fur, and a big brown Labrador hurries over and licks my hands. This only makes the little white dog even more excited and I am smiling and laughing at the same time.

I look over at Daddy and Papa. They are kneeling down, petting a Dalmatian and a medium-sized pit bull, while a tiny brown dog with floppy ears runs wildly around them in one big, happy circle.

I glance around the room and see a warm, cozy place

filled with everything that dogs love. A soft couch is placed along one side of the room, velvety soft dog beds are arranged on the floor, and a wooden dog house stands in the corner of the room. There is even a dog bunk bed with only a few wide stairs leading up to a little bed on top. A basket for dog toys has been knocked over, and most of the toys have been dragged out of the basket and scattered throughout the room. Big, colorful photos in large frames hang on the walls, showing each dog smiling with a worker or volunteer's arms around it. It feels like a loud, fun home filled with love for the dogs in here. It feels perfect.

All of a sudden, the little white puppy jumps up and tries to lick my face and I topple over sideways. The brown Lab sniffs at me with a mixture of concern and insistence that I continue petting him, even in my sideways state.

As I push myself back up to my knees, I see him. A big, brown dog with one big, white spot on his chest. His fur is a deep chestnut brown. He wags his tail happily as he ambles over. I reach my hand out as he kindly bends down to nuzzle my cheek as if to say, *Hey there, you okay?*

This dog is calmer than the others and radiates kindness. My heart melts just looking into his eyes. He sniffs my hand, licks it once, then leans into me, rubbing his head on my hand. I rub the top of his head, behind his ears, then lean over and wrap my arms around his neck, resting my cheek on his soft fur.

I could stay this way forever, but Jazmin directs everyone to head outside. As soon as she opens the door to an outdoor play area, dogs yip and sprint across the field.

We follow and see a wide expanse of open space. A thin layer of snow covers the ground and hangs off the bare branches of the trees.

There are ramps for the dogs to climb on, tunnels to run through, and balance beams made out of tree logs. One little collie dashes from dog to dog, herding them all into a group and then racing them across the field and back.

Jazmin tells us that we can stay and play with the dogs here or grab a leash and take one for a walk along the trail. We decide to go for a walk, so I get a leash and attach it to the brown dog's collar. He has a name tag on his collar that says Spot, so I whisper, "You ready, Spot?"

Daddy has leashed up the pit bull and Papa is struggling to get the little floppy-eared dog to hold still long enough to get its collar on. Spot sits there patiently and waits, looking as though he has all the time in the world.

"Are you sure you can handle that dog all by yourself?" Daddy asks me as we start walking down the trail.

I look down at Spot, who is calmly trotting by my side, and smile up at Daddy. "Yes. We're great! Look how great he is. He's not pulling on the leash or anything. Isn't he just beautiful?"

And it's true. Spot trots happily by my side while Papa's dog constantly races this way and that, getting all tangled up with the leash. I can hear Daddy and Papa chatting, but I'm not really listening. I am mesmerized as I watch Spot walk along the trail. His tail swishes back and forth and his feet plod evenly and effortlessly.

He glances up at me every now and then, and it looks like he is smiling. The look on his doggy face makes me think he's been waiting for this moment with me. Like he knew it would happen and now that it's finally here, he's just loving it, soaking it all in. I feel the same way.

Before I know it, Daddy says it's time to go back, so we turn around and Spot and I jog a little way down the trail. He trots along next to me, not pulling on the leash, but rather staying his calm, gentle self. As soon as Spot and I start jogging, Daddy and Papa's dogs start whining and pulling on their leashes, so soon enough everyone is jogging back down the trail together.

When we reach the outdoor play area, we step through the gate and unhook the dogs' leashes. Spot nuzzles the palm of my hand, and I lean down to pet him again, murmuring, "Good dog, Spot. Good dog."

Daddy chats with Jazmin while I throw a worn tennis ball back and forth for Spot. After a few times, the ball starts to get a little slimy, but I don't mind. Then we run up the ramps, through the tunnels, and across the balance beam logs. More dogs join us and pretty soon there are so many dogs running around after me that I can't even count them all.

Jazmin brings everyone back inside where we give all of the dogs food and water. We listen to her talk about the adoption process while we comb our dogs and say goodbye.

As we're leaving, I hear Jazmin tell my parents, "Your daughter has a passion for dogs. You can just see how much she loves them, and how much they love her."

* * *

For the next few days, I can't stop smiling. I feel like I'm in a dream land where I can't stop thinking about all of the sweet dogs we met. But mostly, about Spot. About his deep brown eyes, soft brown fur, and the way he looks at me with his eyes full of love. I feel something inside of my heart flutter again, like I did on Thanksgiving. But I don't say anything to Daddy or Papa. I just walk around with a great big, giant smile plastered all over my face, and the happiest feeling in the world inside of me.

The feeling stays with me during our math lessons with Maddie the following week. It's with me through reading, lunch, and library time. It follows me home from school, through dinner and bed, and even into my dreams one night. I have a dream where I am swimming in the dark, which would be really scary, but in the dream, it's fun. I am floating through the water peacefully. When I put my head underwater, I see an entire golden world filled with animals living at the bottom of the ocean. But they're not ocean animals, just a golden glow of a city filled with regular animals living under the water. As I watch, one animal glides away from the rest and rises up to meet me. It is a glowing, golden brown dog. An old dog with wise brown eyes who radiates kindness.

When I wake up, I lie in bed not moving for a long time. I hold still and keep my eyes closed, remembering my dream and how peaceful I felt. After a few minutes, I take a deep breath, stretch my legs, and open my eyes with a smile. Orion wakes up and purrs. I pet him gently from his head all the way down to his tail and his rumbly purring gets louder. Finally, I yawn and slide out of bed, trying not to wake him up.

* * *

At science time, Colby tells us that we will be finishing our habitat books to present at parent night in a few weeks. He says there will also be a cultural presentation and our class will be learning a new dance to share with our parents.

Nadine is doing her book on the rain forest habitat. Emery is doing his on the pond habitat, since he loved his close-up experience with the pond at the Labor Day parade. I have already written down my research and what I learned about Arctic foxes, so now I am coloring it all in with pictures of Arctic foxes, polar bears, and snow. Snow is kind of hard to draw, so I choose silver and gray.

Then I fill out the spelling list of words like glacier, hibernate, and permafrost. Some kids are making a bingo game for their books, but I decide to make a memory game for mine. First, I color two pictures of the same animal, then I cut them out into squares and add them to the pile until I have sixteen. I think that is enough for a game of memory. I fold a piece of paper into an envelope and tape it together. Then I stick all of the little squares inside and attach it to the last page on my book. I can't wait to play my memory game with Daddy and Papa when they come to my parent night.

As I work on my project, I keep thinking about Spot at the shelter. I think about how much fun I had with him, how happy I feel thinking about him, and how perfect he would be for our family. I decide that it's time to tell Daddy and Papa what I've been thinking about.

When Papa picks me up from school, however, he says that Daddy is working late again.

"Will he be home for dinner?" I ask.

"No, he won't. He might get home to see you just before you go to bed, but he might not." Papa explains.

I cross my fingers that he does get home in time, but he's still not there when it's time for me to go to sleep. Papa and I call his cell phone as I'm getting tucked into bed, and when Daddy doesn't answer, we leave him a message. "Good night, Daddy! We love you! Hope you are having fun at work!"

Chapter 8

When I wake up in the morning, Daddy is already dressed and ready for work again.

"Morning, Sophie," he says, giving me a quick kiss. "I'm sorry I didn't see you last night. I'll be home earlier tonight, okay?"

I nod and give him a hug. I know they said that they want to work less so we have time to take care of a dog, but this doesn't seem like he is working less at all.

"But why are you—" I start to ask.

Even though he always tells me not to interrupt, Daddy cuts me off. "I'm sorry, Sophie, I can't talk right now. I've gotta run."

"But, Daddy—" I try again.

Daddy looks at something on his phone and says, "Oh man . . . are you kidding me?"

I glare at him as he grabs his keys and rushes out the door, but he doesn't even notice because he's too busy looking at something on his phone.

* * *

On the way to school, Papa gives me good news. "We found out that the shelter we volunteered at is doing a camp over winter break for kids your age. Do you want to go?"

"Yes! Yes, yes, yes!" I yell right away.

Papa laughs and nods his head. "We thought you

would. It's actually good timing because it looks like Daddy and I are both going to be pretty busy at work over the next month."

"Why? Did they not find the bug yet?" I ask. I picture grown-ups crawling on the floor in Daddy's office and peering behind filing cabinets, searching for bugs.

"Well, they fixed the first bug they were working on, but they've found a whole bunch of other bugs that are causing problems," Papa explains. "And the guy who made all the bugs had to quit, so now they're trying to figure out what all he did wrong and they don't have as many people to figure it out. Plus, a lot of people are going on vacation right now and Daddy has to fill in for everyone."

"Papa! When are you guys going to have more time for a dog?" I whine.

Papa glances in the rearview mirror and says gently, "I know it's hard to wait, Sophie. But please try to be patient. I've got a lot of fun holiday orders coming in now, so I'm going to be busier for a while too."

I cross my arms and stare out the window. My frowny face reflects faintly in the window, glaring back at me. We ride the rest of the way to school in silence. I'm so angry that I almost forget about the winter break camp.

We pull up to the hug-and-go and I open my door, ready to storm off. But Papa gets out and pulls me in for a big hug. "We'll sign you up for camp today. I hope you understand that's the best we can do right now. And try to have a good day, sweet pea. I love you."

I stand there and let him kiss the top of my head, then shuffle slowly toward school.

Before I reach the door, Tino sprints up to me and says, "Guess what? We just got a puppy!"

At first, my stomach drops and I feel teardrops prickle behind my eyes like icy daggers. I blink and try to keep the tears from spilling over. How come Tino gets a puppy when he didn't even really want one that much? It's not fair. Dogs are everywhere I look. Everywhere except at my house. And the way things are going, a dog won't be at my house anytime soon.

"You got a puppy?" Emery asks, coming up behind us.

"Yeah, I don't think my mom really wanted one, but this guy my dad works with has a dog who had babies, so my dad decided to get one and surprise her," Tino says. "He said it's an early Christmas present for us."

"Aww . . . what's it look like?" Emery asks.

"He's white, black, and tan and really small. Except his paws; you should see how big his paws are. They're like way too big for him. And he chews on everything! He slept on my bed last night, and when I woke up, he had chewed right through my dad's slipper!" Tino chatters excitedly.

I try to stay mad, but it's actually pretty hard when I start picturing this adorable, little puppy. Pretty soon, I get caught up in the excitement and start to smile. And before I know it, I'm smiling and laughing right along with them.

"Maybe my dad can bring him to school tomorrow when he picks me up so you can see it," Tino continues. "And then when you get a dog, we can have them play

77

together."

By the time I reach my classroom, all I can think about are dogs again. And of course, that makes me think about Spot. Even though I'm still disappointed that my parents are too busy to bring Spot home right now, at least I'll get to see him over winter break. I decide to think about how fun it will be playing with him at camp instead of worrying about my parents' work.

* * *

Later in library time, Aldo reads *Each Kindness* to us, a story about a girl who won't play with a new girl at school. The new girl tries to make friends with Chloe, but Chloe makes fun of her and her old, worn clothes. By the end of the book, I think Chloe realized that she was being mean and wanted to be nicer, but the new girl had already moved away. It makes me sad that Chloe would never get a chance to be nice to the new girl.

When Aldo stops reading and puts down the book, our class is quieter than usual. He looks around and says, "Why do you think Chloe didn't want to be friends with the new girl at first?"

Nadine slowly raises her hand and then says, "I think maybe she was scared because she didn't know why the girl's clothes were old and dirty."

"That's very true," Aldo replies. "Sometimes when we see someone who looks or acts differently, it can be kind of scary at first because we're not used to it. How do you think it made the new girl feel?"

Even Emery remembers to raise his hand before he says, "I think at first, she really wanted to be friends with Chloe and by the end, she was sad but at least she had fun playing by herself."

"Yeah, good," Aldo says and then asks the rest of the class, "What do you wish Chloe could have done differently if she'd had a chance?"

"I wish she would have smiled at the new girl and invited her to play jump rope," I answer. "It doesn't seem fair that by the time she was ready to be friends, the new girl had moved away already."

"Yeah, that's really hard that she didn't get another chance to be a good friend. Sometimes it doesn't always seem like life is fair," he concludes.

I think about that for a long time, even after library time is over.

* * *

Later that night, I finally get my chance to tell Daddy and Papa what I've been thinking about Spot. I tell them about the amazing feeling I have that this will be our dog. I explain how it's just something that I know, deep down in my heart.

"I know you really want a dog, sweetie," Daddy starts slowly. His eyes look tired as he speaks, and he seems kind of distracted. "And we do want to get one for the family eventually, but now is just not a good time."

"Yeah, but I don't want just any dog, Daddy. I want Spot. He's perfect," I implore.

Daddy furrows his eyebrows together and takes a deep breath like he needs extra air to shout.

But before he can say anything, Papa steps in and says, "Let's just take it one step at a time. You'll be spending a lot of time with Spot at camp over winter break, and you'll also get to meet a lot of other dogs while you're there." He takes a deep breath and continues, "This is not a perfect time for our family to get a dog, which means that Spot may not be the perfect dog for us. Someone else could be ready for a dog right now, and if they choose Spot, then he could end up with their family. Remember, we'd love for all of the dogs to get adopted."

My heart sinks so low that I can't even speak. Spot going to another family is unthinkable. At first, my heart feels like it's going to break, shattering into a million pieces. But I remember the feeling of happiness and hope that has settled into my heart lately, and I refuse to let it go. In a rush of anger, I clench my fists and whisper, "He will *not* be going to another family. I know it. I can *feel* it."

Before I realize it, big fat teardrops are running down my face. How can they not understand? Why can't we get him now?

* * *

I don't bring it up again over the next couple of weeks. Daddy continues to leave for work early and stay at work late. As Papa predicted, he starts getting busier with all of his holiday work too. I am spending more and more days after school at Nadine's since no one is home at my house.

Usually, I love spending time with Nadine after school. But lately, it makes me sad since I know it's only because my parents are working too much. I think about Spot and wonder how he is doing at the shelter. I try not to think about him getting adopted and instead try to focus on seeing him over winter break. But it's hard. Some days, I feel like we're never going to get a dog.

I think Nadine and her parents have noticed that I've been feeling down lately. Sometimes they try to distract me or crack a joke. But sometimes they know that I need some quiet space to read a book and think my own thoughts.

Today Nadine invited Emery over to her house too. Emery celebrates Hanukkah, so he brought over vegetable potato latkes to share with us. We are huddled around Nadine's dining room table munching on warm latkes. Pia is snacking on raisins with one hand and has a latke in her other. As she eats, she happily puts her raisins in a pile. She keeps asking for more and more raisins to add to her pile.

Nadine's mom made cinnamon-spiced apple cider and it makes the whole house smell delicious. The food, warmth, music, and friends all take away some of my sadness and make me smile.

Emery is studying Pia and declares, "She looks like she's playing a dreidel game."

Nadine and I look at him questioningly, so he explains, "You have to spin the dreidel and try to collect all of the game pieces from the pot. A game piece can be anything small, like a nut or a coin. Or a raisin." He pulls a dreidel out of his backpack. "Each side of the dreidel says something different, like put a game piece into the pot, take everything, take half of the pot, give half of your pot, or nothing. Pia looks like she won the game with all of those raisins in front of her."

We all grab a handful of raisins and invite Pia to play too, but she doesn't want to give up any of her raisins. So we let her watch us as she eats. Every time someone wins something from the pot, Pia shouts until we give her a raisin. Then she happily adds it to her pile and continues to watch us. Emery says if you win, you're encouraged to share your whole pot with other people, especially if you're playing with coins.

I love the game and am having so much fun, I can't believe when Papa comes in and says it's time to leave. He looks cold and a little out of breath, but agrees to sit down for a mug of cider and one round of the dreidel game before we go home. We all excitedly explain the rules and warn him not to take any raisins from Pia's pile. While we play, I see him start to relax and smile a little. I climb up on his lap and cheer when he gets a game piece.

As we walk home, my worries fall far behind me and I feel happier than I have in a while.

* * *

Finally, it is time for our parent night and our mid-year presentations. The school is packed and parents crowd the halls. Loud voices buzz all around me, making it hard to hear.

Papa and I are here already, and Daddy said he will be here a little bit late. I show Papa my habitat book and we play the memory game I created. It's fun, but I wish Daddy were here to play it with us too. We also walk around and look at the other habitat books in my class. We play some of the other habitat games like bingo that the other students made.

Everything is wonderful, except that Daddy still isn't here. Finally, it's time to do the dance that Colby taught us. We go up on the stage behind the curtain. The music comes on and the curtain goes up. I take my place in the dance and twirl, whirl, and jump my way across the stage.

At the end of our dance, we line up across the stage to take a bow and that's when I look out in the audience and see Daddy sitting next to Papa. He *is* here. He saw my dance. I bow and a smile opens up on my face and moves down into my heart, where it settles itself as though it had been there the whole time and never left. And with that, the night is over and we bundle into puffy jackets, scarves, and hats, and disperse into the bitter cold.

Chapter 9

As Papa promised, I go to the dog camp over winter break. I guess it's not just a dog camp because there are so many other animals there—cats, guinea pigs, and rabbits. But I am most excited about spending time with the dogs and seeing how Spot is doing.

On the first day, Papa leads me to a room in the animal shelter that has yellow walls and white tables arranged in a big square in the center. He signs me in, then quickly says goodbye. I know I have been so excited to come, but now that I'm here I realize that I don't know anyone. Suddenly, I feel a lump in my throat and I look down at the floor. I walk quietly over to a table and sit down. I keep my eyes focused on the ground, and sit there twirling the end of my shirt in my hands over and over. I miss Daddy and Papa. I miss being in a class with Nadine and Emery. I can't remember why I agreed to come.

Slowly, the room starts to fill up and I can hear other kids saying goodbye to their parents and chatting and laughing with each other. Two friends sit together on the other side of the table. When I glance up, I see kids talking in big groups around the table.

But there's also one boy who looks a little bit younger than me, sitting quietly with his head down a few seats away. As I watch him, he looks up and we both smile and then look down right away again. I wonder if he feels as nervous as I do.

We both sit there quietly for a few more minutes, and then the camp counselors sit down and start talking. We play a game to break the ice. When we introduce ourselves, we also have to say the name of an animal that starts with the same letter as our first name. When it gets to my turn, I take a deep breath and quietly say that my name is Sophie and I love Spot, the dog I met volunteering here over Thanksgiving. The shy boy goes next and says his name is Hayes and he has a pet hamster named Hammy that he really loves. He looks relieved when he is done talking, and I give him an encouraging smile.

We stay in the sunny, yellow room all morning, learning how to take care of the animals and doing crafts. We tie string, bells, and feathers onto a stick to make a cat toy. Then it's time to meet the animals. The counselors divide us into two groups so it won't be as overwhelming for the animals to have everyone meet them all at once.

Hayes and I are in the same group. I decide to do something brave, so I walk over and say, "Hi, um . . . how old is Hammy?"

Immediately, his face lights up and he doesn't look as nervous anymore. "He just turned two. That's actually pretty old for a hamster. I heard that turtles can live for forty years though!"

When he stops talking, he looks down again and shuffles his feet.

"Wow, that's cool," I say encouragingly. "We live by a creek and I saw a turtle in it once. It was a really big one."

Hayes doesn't say anything, so I stretch my arms out

in a big circle and add, "Like, really big. My dad said it was a snapping turtle."

Hayes looks up then and smiles briefly before shuffling his feet again.

Helping Hayes open up makes me feel more confident, because I know I'm not the only one who feels shy meeting new people.

"Okay, guys, follow me," Jazmin—the lady with curly hair and a bright smile—tells us and leads our group out of the room.

"Come on," I tell Hayes. "I met Jazmin here after Thanksgiving, and you better walk fast to keep up."

Hayes and I practically jog after her and follow our group through a door at the end of the hallway. The cat room is similar to the dog room, except filled with things that cats love.

"Ooh, green is my favorite color!" Hayes exclaims, looking at the walls, which are painted a pastel shade of green.

"We try to make the room comfortable for our animal friends, and we've found that light green helps keep the cats relaxed and happy," Jazmin explains. "We also have a small, pastel blue room in the back for cats who need some space away from the group. We only let one or two cats in there at a time."

Similar to the dog room, there is a framed picture of each cat hanging on the wall. I look around the green room. It is wide and open with cats and kittens wandering freely around. Some cats are snuggled up together, napping on cat beds. Others are climbing tall cat towers or sitting on little shelves on the wall. A calico cat is scratching its claws on a cat scratcher in the corner of the room.

I watch as a gray kitten takes a flying leap from the top of his cat house and lands at our feet, jumping up to bat at the feathers on the cat toy I made this morning. I jangle the toy to the left and the kitten pounces to the left. Then I spin around and move it back to the right and quick as a flash, he spins around and pounces again. This time, he catches it with his paws and sits down on the feather. Holding it with one paw, he leans back and licks his other paw to clean his ear. Then he shakes his head, leaps back onto the cat toy, and grabs the feather with his mouth. He tugs and pulls the toy out of my hands. He carries the toy a few feet away and settles down to lick the feather, purring contentedly.

Hayes and I look at each other and laugh. Pretty soon another cat strolls by and since the kitten still has my toy, Hayes shakes his cat toy and lets this cat chase it back and forth.

We spend the rest of the morning petting and playing with the cats. We are having so much fun that I almost forget how much I wanted to see Spot. But as soon as it's time for our group to visit the dogs, I jump up and clap my hands. We enter the dog room and I feel like I never left. I quickly scan the room. To my relief, I find Spot lounging on a dog bed in the back of the room. He gets up and trots over to me with that same sweet smile on his face. I bend down and scratch behind his ears, then pet his back gently.

As I pet him, I look around the room and see all sorts of new dogs that weren't here last time. I look for the pit bull that Daddy walked when we were here and the floppy-eared brown dog that Papa walked, and I don't see either of them. Jazmin explains that a lot of dogs have already been adopted, but there are still so many dogs who need a forever home.

When it's time to play outside, we stay in the outdoor play area instead of walking down the trail. I throw a ball back and forth for Spot, and Hayes races up and down the ramps with three little dogs yipping and leaping after him. Before I know it, the day is over and I have to say goodbye to Spot again.

"I'll see you tomorrow," I whisper.

* * *

The rest of the week flies by in a blur of crafts, lessons on animal care, and playtime. Hayes and I gradually shed our shyness like lizards shed their skin. Every day, more and more pets come to the shelter and more are adopted out. But every day I come in, Spot is always there waiting for me. I am beginning to think of him as my dog, and I think I can get used to him living here as long as I can come visit.

I even asked if I could volunteer here on the weekends after camp is done and both Daddy and Papa agreed. When I told Hayes, he said he'd ask his parents if he could volunteer after camp too.

On the last day of camp, I don't feel nervous at all. Right away, Hayes and I find each other and start chatting about everything we want to do for the last day of camp. Hayes is excited because he heard the shelter just got a turtle and that's pretty rare.

When we get a chance to see the turtle, she is really cute. This turtle is about the size of both of my fists put together—much smaller than the one I saw by the creek. She is in a glass tank with a little pool surrounded by rocks, dirt, and plants. It's a pretty big tank, so we watch as the little turtle swims playfully back and forth across her pool. Then she waggles her feet back and forth and pulls herself up on a rock. She stretches her neck way out of her shell and takes a big bite of a leaf.

"Nellie is a young turtle," one of the counselors explains. I look at her wrinkled face and neck and think that she looks kind of old. I guess that's how all turtles look. Nellie is so sweet and kind of funny, and I realize both Hayes and I are grinning from ear to ear. We look at each other and laugh.

During craft time, we make dog chew toys out of old T-shirts. I choose red, white, and green and decide to give mine to Spot as a Christmas gift. When I show it to him, he tugs on it and happily slobbers all over it. Spending time with Spot has been the best Christmas present ever.

* * *

The night before school starts up again after winter

break, it starts snowing. I keep asking and asking Papa if it means that we won't have school tomorrow, but he just says, "We'll see."

When I wake up in the morning, the world is white and beautiful, but only covered with a few inches of snow. I don't think it's enough to cancel school, but I grab a book and snuggle down under my covers anyway.

A few minutes later, Papa sticks his head in my room. "Time to get moving, Sophie. Up and at 'em."

Later at school, Magnolia and Maddie, the math dog, stroll into class, bundled up in matching knit sweaters. Maddie snuffles loudly as she greets us, and Magnolia declares, "I think Maddie is so happy to be back in school with you!"

Seeing Maddie all snuggled up in her soft sweater makes me happy to be back in school too. We're learning about perimeters, so Magnolia hands out rectangle blocks to everyone in the class. We line them up around the room to make huge shapes. Maddie walks around with us as we take turns measuring each side. Magnolia helps us with the measuring tape and writes the numbers on the board so we can add up each side to find out the total perimeter of the shape.

* * *

At library time, I snuggle down on the rug and lean back against a pillow. I gaze up at the papier-mâché dragon and clouds hanging from the ceiling and relax as Aldo starts to read.

I love listening to Aldo read. He always chooses the best books and his voice changes with the characters and the tone of the book to bring us right into the story. Today he is reading *And Tango Makes Three*. I love the book from the moment I see the cover, because the baby penguin is so cute.

As he reads, I love the story even more because it reminds me of me and Daddy and Papa. The story is about two daddy penguins named Roy and Silo who lived in Central Park Zoo in New York and wanted to have a baby penguin so much that they brought an egg-shaped rock into their nest and tried to hatch it. Obviously, that didn't work, so one of the zookeepers gave them an egg that another pair of penguins couldn't take care of. Roy and Silo took turns keeping the egg warm until it hatched into a baby penguin named Tango.

I am so happy that Roy and Silo were able to have their own baby at the end of the story, because I can tell that they wanted one so much. And Tango is so fluffy and cute!

I feel special when I read it, because it also reminds me of how much Daddy and Papa wanted me to join their family. They had to wait for years before I was adopted. First, Papa wanted to have a baby, but Daddy wasn't sure they were ready. Finally, Daddy agreed. Then they still had to wait until the adoption agency could find them a baby. I'm glad they ended up waiting, because it means that they found me.

I am thinking *and Sophie makes three* in my head when I realize that we actually have five of us in our family when you count Artemis and Orion. Then I think *and Spot makes six* and hope that it comes true without having to wait too much longer.

Chapter 10

Saturday morning is my first morning as a regular volunteer at the animal shelter. All of the snow has melted, turning the outdoor play area into a muddy field. The dogs don't seem to mind. Mud clings to their legs and bellies. They race from one end of the field and back, flicking mud this way and that when they spin around. Even Spot, who is usually so calm, zips around the field with a look of glee on his face. He brings me a soggy tennis ball covered with mud, drops it at my feet, and looks up at me like he's just given me the best present I could have ever hoped for. I reach down and pick it up. I throw it as far as I can and muddy water sprays off it in a long arc.

When Hayes gets there, he waves and walks over to me. As he gets closer, his eyes get wide and then he laughs.

"Wow, um, nice hair," he says with a little laugh.

I reach up and realize there is a big glob of mud in my hair. I shrug and laugh too.

"You should see Spot. He's covered in mud!" I respond.

As if on cue, Spot trots over, drops the ball in front of us, and shakes wet, muddy clumps with a renewed sense of vigor and enjoyment. He is positively beaming. I bend down to pet him, smearing mud through his fur and in between the fingers of my gloves. "Good boy! You're having so much fun!"

A gray puppy bounds over, barks, and puts his front

paws up on Hayes's knees. He reaches down and pets the puppy's soft ears. "Aww, you're soft as silk."

Pretty soon, both dogs are chasing each other back and forth across the play area, racing after the tennis ball. Hayes and I toss the ball over and over again until Spot finally trudges over to me and plops down tiredly. He doesn't seem to mind that he is lying down right in the mud. I kneel down and pet his head, then lead him inside to his water bowl.

After Spot takes a long, sloppy drink, Jazmin laughs and gives us that big, friendly smile that she always seems to have.

"Come on, let's get Spot washed up," she says and hurries inside.

I try to walk as quickly as I can without slipping, but I can't keep up with her.

At the end of the hall, she stops and holds the door open for me and Spot. The doggie bathing room smells like wet dog and a minty kind of soap. Spot hops easily into the bath, and Jazmin pulls her curly, brown hair back in a bun and shows me how to bathe him. Spot loves the warm water as much as he loved getting all muddy, and he paws the water back and forth, making little splashes in the bath. Now I'm dripping wet, which makes mud run down my clothes.

Before long, Spot steps out of the bath looking like a much smaller version of himself with his fur plastered down to his sides. Before I can grab a towel to rub him dry, Spot shakes vigorously, spraying water everywhere. Then he leans into me so forcefully that I almost fall over. When we're all done, Spot's brown fur is gleaming. It is smooth and beautiful, and makes him look more radiant than ever. When Papa arrives to take me home, he smiles and shakes his head. Daddy, on the other hand, does not respond well when I walk into the house.

"Sophie! Please, stop! You are dripping wet and you're leaving a trail of mud down the hallway!" he shouts irritably.

"Sorry, Daddy, I'm taking my shoes off," I apologize. "You should have seen Spot, though. He was so much worse! We had to give him a bath and everything. They taught me how to bathe him, so I know I can totally do it when we get a dog. Can we get a dog, Daddy?"

Daddy ignores my smile, then turns quickly around, leaving me with only a short, "No."

I watch as he disappears up the stairs, suddenly feeling an icy chill settle into my stomach.

"And grab a rag and wipe up that mud!" Daddy shouts over his shoulder as he turns the corner into his office.

* * *

On Monday, our class goes on a field trip to the fire station. It is warm and sunny. I don't even need my hat or gloves on the walk there.

As we go through the door, we're greeted by Charlie, the fire station dog. He is a big, brown dog who sits patiently by the firefighters as we line up to pet him. When it's my turn, I run my hand from his head all the way down his back, and he happily wags his tail.

First, we sit in a room inside that looks kind of like a classroom. Except there aren't as many colorful decorations in this room as there are in all of the classrooms at my school. The walls are white and there is a long whiteboard across one wall. The only splash of color comes from a flag in the corner of the room.

The tables are made for adults, and when I sit on the chair, my feet swing from side to side without touching the floor.

A firefighter steps to the front of the room. "Good morning! My name is Katrina and I'm going to ask you a few safety questions before we go see the fire trucks. Who's excited to see the trucks?"

Everyone cheers.

"Okay, first. Where should you go if there's a fire?"

That one's easy. We have fire drills at school and always go to the playground. Hands shoot into the air, and Katrina calls on Nadine.

"Outside!"

"Yes, great." Katrina nods. "Now, what do you do if you can't open the door to get outside?"

That question's harder. I look around at the rest of the class. No one raises their hand.

Katrina helps us out. "If you can't get out, find a window to stand by because that's the first place we're going to look for you when we get there to fight the fire."

I didn't know that, but now that I think about it, that makes sense.

"Okay, how many of you know your phone number?" Hands shoot into the air again. Almost everyone has their hand up.

"Good. And how many of you know your address?"

I start to raise my hand, but then stop. I know I live in Lafayette, Colorado in America, but I forget the rest. I look around the room. Nearly everyone has their hand in the air.

"Good job. I want you all to go home and practice your address and phone number," Katrina instructs. "Now, who knows what to do if there's a lot of smoke in the house already?"

"You have to get down really low, like on your belly and crawl out," Tino answers.

"Yep, that's right. We're going to practice right now. Would you like to show us how to do it?"

Tino nods eagerly and hops out of his chair. The rest of the class quickly follows and we crawl along the floor to the door. Our teacher, Colby, even crawls with us.

We crawl through the door and then stand up as we enter the garage where they park the fire trucks. The air smells like diesel and smoke. Kind of like a gas station and a campfire mixed into one. I look up and see the tallest ceiling I've ever seen in my whole life. It's so tall that a giraffe could fit in here.

The firefighters tell us about the tools on the trucks, and then we get to climb up inside. The fire truck is so big that I feel like I am climbing a mountain just to get inside. I scoot through the cab of the truck to the other side, and another firefighter holds on to me as I jump down. It feels like I'm flying.

When I land, I'm smiling from ear to ear. Charlie is surrounded by a circle of students, all eagerly petting him. The way he stands there patiently, soaking in all of the attention with all the patience in the world, reminds me of Spot. I bet Spot would love it here.

"Does Charlie get to ride in the fire truck?" Emery asks.

"Yeah, sometimes he comes with us," a firefighter responds. "Not all the time, but sometimes."

Finally, we walk outside and the firefighters open a fire hydrant. Water shoots so far out that it soaks the sidewalk halfway down the block! We jump up and down, screaming and clapping our hands. I had no idea that so much water could come out of there so quickly!

After that, we thank the firefighters, say goodbye, and walk back to school, chatting noisily about what a great field trip it was!

* * *

A few days later, it's cold again. That's how it is in the winter in Colorado—one day it will be warm enough to leave your jacket at home and the next day it will be a snow storm. When I wake up, I look outside and all I see is snow. The trees are covered in it. The cars are hidden under large piles of snow. Our patio chairs and barbeque are indistinct bumps of snow several feet tall. The roads are coated so thick it looks like they are fields of rolling hills, not streets where cars could drive. And there is still snow coming down.

I wander downstairs for breakfast.

Papa looks up from his tea and smiles. "Guess what, sweet pea? It's a snow day; no school today. And good news—I'm done with my holiday and New Year's projects and work is starting to settle down, which means I can take the day off with you too."

"Yes!" I shout, jumping up to do a little happy dance around the kitchen.

Papa smiles and we both bounce around the kitchen giddily, whooping it up. When Daddy walks in, he looks at us, shakes his head, and smiles, but doesn't join in. Papa and I keep dancing and jumping around, laughing until our sides ache.

Daddy grabs a bagel to eat upstairs in his office, and eventually Papa and I settle down into a breakfast of scrambled eggs with mushrooms, spinach, and cheese. Papa puts habanero hot sauce all over his and then pretends to be a fire-breathing dragon. "Quick! Quick! Somebody bring the water!" he shouts, pretending to clutch his throat.

I giggle and point to his water glass right in front of him. He grabs it and gulps it down noisily. "Whew! That was a close one! The dragon almost burned down the whole city!"

I smile, and then remember our field trip to the fire station. Now that I'm home, I can remember our address easily.

"I forgot our address yesterday," I tell Papa while we eat.

He nods. "Yeah, sometimes that happens. We'll practice it again today. We'll even have a treasure hunt today to find the pieces of our address outside."

I stare at him blankly.

"Did you know that the number part of our address is on our house, and the street part of our address is on the street sign?" he elaborates.

"Oh, yeah . . ." I say, thinking it over.

Papa quizzes me a few times, and I repeat our address easily. After breakfast, we bundle up in snowsuits, snow boots, hats, and gloves.

I step outside and look at the side of our house. Sure enough, there are dark brown numbers carved out of wood hanging on the side of our house by the garage. I look toward the tall, green street sign on the corner. Icy currents swirl down the street, and snow covers part of the sign, hiding the name of the street.

Papa and I tromp through the snow toward the corner. The snow is up to my knees in some places. Every step feels like I'm climbing over miles and miles of sand dunes. I wonder if we are ever going to make it to the corner. It feels like we have been hiking for hours when we finally reach the street sign. Papa tries and tries to jump up to brush off the snow, but the sign is too tall.

Instead, he picks up a tree branch that fell down and brushes off the snow with it. When I can read the name of the street, Papa quizzes me one last time. Now if I forget, I can just picture the name on the sign and remember it easier.

We trudge back to the front yard and start building a snow fort. The snow is slightly wet, which makes great packing snow and our fort escalates into a double walled fortress with walls that come up to my shoulders and a snowman family standing guard out front.

We are making a pile of snowballs when Nadine and her dogs trek over to us through the snow. The littlest dog, Luna, sprints toward our fort and takes a flying leap, landing in a soft pile of snow. Patch and Ginger follow closely behind, nipping at falling snowflakes and rolling around in the deep, soft snow.

Nadine and I toss them snowballs and laugh as they jump up, trying to eat them. Papa stands up and waves at Nadine's mom, Cordelia, who is slowly making her way toward us through the snow. Nadine's dad, Marcelo, trails behind, pulling Pia in a wooden sled. Pia is bundled up so warm that it looks like she might not even be able to move her arms, and I doubt she could walk even if she tried. Instead, she leans back in her little sled, watching everyone around her with a look of amazement on her face.

Nadine and I alternate between adding snowballs to our pile in the fort and tossing them to the dogs. Before long, we have a huge stash of snowballs and we begin to plot our strategy. Since Nadine's entire family is already outside, we decide to attack Daddy when he comes out. We stash some of the snowballs in front next to the attack fort, then move back and save the rest for the retreat fort in back.

We add more snow to each fortress, making sure that

there's enough support for the walls. After a while, we get tired and hungry. Daddy still hasn't come outside, so we leave the snowballs and traipse slowly inside.

We tug off our frozen clothes and drop them in a pile by the door. Papa serves everyone hot tea and tostadas. Daddy comes downstairs to greet everyone, but says he can only stay for a little bit before he has to go back upstairs and keep working.

"Daddy, will you come outside with us after lunch?" I ask, trying not to sound too whiny.

"I don't know, Sophie. It depends on how quickly I can finish what I'm working on," Daddy says, frowning.

I try not to slump down too much in my chair, saying instead, "Well, just for a little bit this afternoon. Please?"

"We'll see," he says without smiling. Papa hands him a plate, and he excuses himself to head back upstairs.

After lunch, Nadine stays at my house to play. We spend all afternoon coloring in activity books, doing puzzles, and playing games. I tell her about volunteering with Spot, about making friends with Hayes, and about how busy Daddy has been lately.

"It's not fair that he has to work so much now," I complain. "Especially when he said he wants to slow down and have time for a dog. But now when I see him, he's always grumpy and doesn't want to listen to me."

Nadine nods slowly, then says, "I'm sorry, Sophie. At least Papa has time to play."

That is true, I realize. I hadn't thought about that since I've been so upset about Daddy working all the time.

Maybe we only need Papa to work less so we can get a dog. I decide I'll ask him about it later.

* * *

As the afternoon light fades to a light gray, I bundle up in my snow gear again to walk Nadine home. We step outside and shiver against the cold. A trail of footprints makes a path through the deep snow, which makes it a little easier to walk through. Before we get too far, though, we hear the door to our house open and then close again.

We look back and see Daddy and Papa both bundled up in snow pants, hats, and gloves with a look of excitement on their faces. "Hurry! To the fortress!" they shout.

Quick as a flash, Nadine and I race back to our attack fort and grab a snowball as the first snowball sails over our heads.

"We're going to get you!" I shout, and throw a snowball as fast as I can.

It hits the side of the house and smashes to pieces. Daddy packs another snowball and lobs it toward us. It sails over the snow fort wall and smacks my shoulder as I try to duck.

"Aha! You can't get away that easily!" Daddy shouts with a smile.

Nadine throws another snowball and it looks like she's going to hit Papa's leg this time, but he reaches down and catches it. "Foiled!" he shouts, grinning, and takes aim at us again.

Nadine and I are rapidly running out of snowballs. "Retreat! Retreat!" I shout, and we scurry back to our retreat fort where our final stash of snowballs reside.

Snowballs from Daddy and Papa come thundering against our fortress wall as we duck safely behind. Finally, Nadine lands a hit right on Daddy's belly and we high five each other. Pretty soon, everyone has run out of snowballs and we call a truce.

"You guys did an amazing job building these forts today," Daddy compliments us.

"I didn't think you were going to see them," I admit.

He shrugs and says, "I'm almost done with my work, and I really didn't want to miss seeing your amazing snow forts. Papa said you guys worked really hard on them today." Then he adds thoughtfully, "They really do look great. I can't believe how tall the walls are. Makes me feel like a kid again."

Daddy smiles and gives me a hug. "Now let's get Nadine home and get back inside before we all freeze."

Chapter 11

On Saturday at the shelter, I overhear Jazmin talking about how many pets have been adopted recently. When I look around, I realize it's true. There were so many dogs here last week that aren't here anymore, and new ones have arrived. The gray puppy that Hayes and I played with last week isn't here. An adorable chocolate Lab is stretched out on one of the dog beds, snuggled between a chew toy and a poodle that I've never seen before.

Then I realize that I don't see Spot either. I walk around and around the room, peering in all of the dog houses and on the dog beds, even the ones that I know Spot doesn't like. I even walk over to the window and look outside on the play area, even though I know that no dogs should be out there yet. Spot isn't there either.

When I turn around, Jazmin comes over and tells me that Spot wasn't feeling well and is with the shelter vet right now. I ask when I can see him and she tells me that as soon as the vet is done with his examination, she'll let me know.

"Why is Spot with the vet?" I ask, worry written all over my face. "Is he okay?"

"Spot has been with us a long time. And sometimes when a dog stays at a shelter too long, his spirit starts to get broken. Spot is one of our oldest dogs, and sometimes that makes it hard for a dog to be adopted," she explains.

"Yeah, but every time I see him, he's doing really well.

He's always happy to see me and play with me," I counter.
She smiles then. "I've noticed that. You two really seem to have a connection. Spot lights up when you come." She pauses. "But when you're not here, I think he gets really lonely. Some days, he only wants to sleep in the corner of the room. He won't get up to play with the other dogs, and he's starting to eat less and less every day. We think living in the shelter for so long is starting to take its toll on Spot. But we're having the vet check him out to make sure he's not sick. They should be finishing up soon, and we'll let you know what the vet says, okay?"

I nod, thoughts swirling around inside my head. *What if Spot keeps getting worse? What if he's also sick? How do I make him feel better?*

Spot doesn't join the group until we're already outside. He doesn't look like he wants to be outside, wandering slowly around in a corner by the door. When the worker closes the door, Spot whines and then slumps onto the ground in a heap.

I run over and shout, "Spot! Hey, Spot! There you are! I'm so happy to see you!"

When Spot hears my voice, his ears prick up and as soon as he sees me running toward him, he jumps to his feet and bounds over to me, tail wagging.

"See? You're okay. You're going to be just fine," I tell him soothingly, as much to reassure myself as him. Tears are glistening at the corner of my eyes, threatening to spill over.

I try to pet him and give him a big hug, but by now he's

so excited, he prances this way and that and won't stay still. I laugh and wipe away a stray tear that escaped down my cheek. He spies his favorite ball next to the fence, races over to pick it up in his mouth, and sprints back to drop it at my feet.

"Okay, okay," I tell him, laughing. "I get it. You're ready to play."

Jazmin sees us playing and strolls over to tell me that the vet didn't find anything wrong with Spot. "Physically, he's doing fine. That's the good news. The hard part is now we need to figure out what else we can do to keep his spirits up. And make sure that he keeps eating enough."

* * *

As soon as Papa picks me up, I frantically tell him about Spot. "I'm so worried, Papa. When I see him, he's fine. We have so much fun together. He always wags his tail and plays ball with me. He loves this one ball; it's his favorite. And he'll chase it back and forth across the field like he could run all day long. Why wouldn't he be like that when I'm gone? He went to the vet and everything, but he's not sick. Jazmin thinks he's just sad, because he hasn't been adopted yet. What are we going to do?"

"Okay, sweetie, remember to take a breath every now and then. I can tell you're really upset about it, and I know this is really scary for you. Let's take it one step at a time." Papa gives me a reassuring smile, but I don't feel reassured. I still picture Spot huddled in a corner all by himself.

"First of all, it's good that the vet checked him out and there's nothing else going on. They take really good care of the dogs there. And second, it's true that dogs who have been in a shelter longer can become sad and withdrawn. Even though it's an amazing shelter, the dogs need a deeper level of connection than they typically get at a shelter. Dogs need a consistent family, lots of love, and lots of exercise to really thrive long term. That's why they try to find every pet a forever family," he explains gently.

"I know, but what are we going to do?" I press him again. I am trying to keep my face from crumbling, but I feel tears prickling at the corner of my eyes again.

"Keep going to volunteer. It sounds like Spot really likes having you around."

I nod, though a few tears leak down my face. I wipe them away with my sleeve.

"Then maybe it's time for Daddy and me to talk about our timeline again. This is certainly earlier than we anticipated, and Daddy's still got a lot going on at work right now. But we were hoping that after the big project he's working on wraps up, we could start focusing on slowing down."

Papa glances at my face, then cautions, "I know we've talked about it before, Sophie, and you need to remember that as scary as this feels with Spot, we're not going to rush into anything. It won't be a good fit for us unless we're all ready to have a dog. We might still have to wait awhile, okay?"

"Okay," I mumble. I cross my fingers, though, and

wish up to the stars and back that Daddy and Papa say we can get a dog soon. That we can adopt Spot before he gets worse.

* * *

The following Sunday is my birthday party. I'm turning nine years old today, and my family and friends are all coming over to celebrate.

Daddy and Papa let me open one present last night, a game of pin the tail on the donkey. As soon as everyone arrives this afternoon, we set it up and spin each other around and around. Emery's tail is actually really close to the donkey. So is Tino's. Nadine's tail is way off the poster on the wall. Hayes made it on the poster, but only on the grass that the donkey is standing on. We let Pia take a turn, even though she pushes the bandana up on top of her head and sticks the tail right where she wants it. She chooses the donkey's back, and we all laugh.

Finally, it's my turn and they spin me around and around. I lean to one side as I wobble toward the wall. Then I plant the tail down as hard as I can, and when I take the bandana off my face, I see that it's pinned right to the donkey's face!

After we're tired of playing, we sit down at the table for banana bread muffins.

"Another year older, another year wiser," Papa says with a smile as he sets a muffin in front of me on my special birthday plate. I smile as he lights the candles and everyone sings "Happy Birthday." Then I close my eyes, take a deep breath, and blow out the candles.

As Daddy hands out muffins, I tell my friends what I wished for. It was actually two wishes. First, that Spot gets better. And second, that we can give him a forever home.

As we eat, Gramps leans over and says, "I hear you really want a dog, Sophie."

I nod vigorously, but can't say anything because my mouth is full.

"Do you know that when your Papa was a little boy, he had a dog too?"

I shake my head and swallow. "He did? What was it like?"

"Oh, it was the most rambunctious little fellow. A brown little pup that jumped up and down all day long. It had even more energy than your Papa did when he was a boy." Gramps's eyes twinkle like they do when he tells a good story.

"We would play with him and race him back and forth all day long, but that dog never ran out of energy. Until the evening. He would follow Papa and Uncle Leopold upstairs at bedtime, and curl himself into a ball at the end of the bed. Sometimes he'd choose Papa's bed and sometimes he'd choose Leopold's bed. If he started favoring one kid over the other, oh, they would raise a stink about it," Gramps says, chuckling. "Then me or Nana would have to go upstairs and sort it out so they could go to sleep."

I try to picture that. Papa getting all worked up over his dog sleeping on Uncle Leopold's bed, not his.

"That's only half of the story, Dad!" Uncle Leopold interjects. "When the pup would settle down on my bed, Augustus would try to coax him over to his bed! He'd even sneak dog biscuits upstairs in his pockets at bedtime, then he'd whistle and wave a dog biscuit around in front of the pup's nose to make him choose his bed. It really wasn't fair!"

I look to Papa, who has a faraway look on his face. "Oh man, I haven't thought about that in a long time. You're right, though, Leopold, I wanted that little dog to sleep on my bed so much. I was always so sad when he chose to sleep with you."

Then Papa laughs and adds, "But you're right, that wasn't very fair of me to try to sneak him away from you. If I recall correctly, though, that only happened once or twice before Mom and Dad caught on and straightened me out. Plus, that dog was always playing with you during the day. Even though I'm older, I couldn't keep up with you two, so I was trying to make up for lost time."

Uncle Leopold's face softens and he smiles wistfully. "Yeah, we used to play outside all day long, running in the field, jumping over logs, building forts . . . and that dog went everywhere with us. Man, I miss that little guy."

I look over at Daddy and ask, "Did you have a dog when you were little, too, Daddy?" I love hearing stories about when Daddy and Papa were kids.

Daddy shakes his head. "No, but I did have two cats. And a rabbit. The cats were great fun to play with, and that little rabbit was so soft. He was white with black spots, and he would eat all of my leftover vegetables that I'd put in his cage. We had a special bond in that way," he says with a chuckle. "I was really good at feeding him, but I was never very good at keeping his cage clean. Even though I promised that I would be, Mum had to do most of it herself."

"If we get Spot, Daddy, don't worry, I *will* take care of him," I declare. "The most. You won't have to do it all yourself."

Daddy's lips form a tight smile, but he doesn't say anything. I can tell that he doesn't quite believe me.

Chapter 12

A few days later at school, we are learning about the scientific method in science class. Colby says the scientific method will help us learn how to study the world around us. The scientific method is a series of steps: question, research, hypothesis, experiment, analysis, and conclusion.

We already have a question that we're working on as a class: will different seeds from the same plant grow the same way as all the other seeds? We already learned the different parts of plants and what they do. And we read that all plants need soil, water, oxygen, and sun to grow. Colby says that step was our research. Now we have to come up with a hypothesis, which is basically a guess of what we think the answer will be.

I know that babies of all species tend to have similar characteristics as their parents. But not all siblings are exactly the same. I don't have a brother or sister, so I don't have anything to compare it to personally. But Nadine's little sister has black hair and dark brown skin just like her. They look a lot alike, except her sister has dark green eyes and Nadine has dark brown eyes.

Since I was adopted, I didn't get my looks from either Daddy or Papa. Daddy is big and tall with strong arms. He has straight, blond hair that sometimes gets in his eyes when he forgets to cut it.

Papa is shorter than Daddy and has darker skin to

match his dark brown hair. Papa's hair is thick and wavy, but not as curly as mine. Right now it's just long enough to tuck behind his ears. Sometimes it's long enough to pull into a ponytail, and other times he cuts it so short the waves almost disappear. I cried the first time he cut his long ponytail, but now I'm used to it either way.

My hair is brown, long, and super curly. I also have freckles all over my face. Neither Daddy nor Papa have freckles.

Even though we don't look the same, I think being in a family makes you act the same. Sometimes Daddy and I run around the house acting goofy and he says we have the same funny bone. I know that's not a real bone in my body, but I agree that we both have it. Except that we don't goof off as much anymore since Daddy is so busy with work.

"Okay, let's read the hypotheses that you've written down," Colby announces, startling me back to the assignment.

I quickly scribble a guess that all of the seeds will grow leaves that are the same color.

"I'll go," Tino says, raising his hand. Colby nods and he continues, "I think some plants will have more leaves than others."

"Good guess," Colby says. "That's a great hypothesis."

Next Nadine says, "I think the ones closest to the window will grow the tallest, because they'll get more sun."

"Excellent," Colby states. "Next?"

Emery tentatively raises his hand. "Maybe some won't grow at all?"

"Hmm . . . interesting guess. That could be. We'll have to wait and see," Colby responds. Then he asks the class, "Do you think all of the seeds will grow at the same speed as the others?"

I raise my hand. "No, I think some will grow faster."

"Okay, these are all great guesses. The next step is fun," Colby states. "We're going to make an experiment to test our hypotheses. Everyone gets to choose one bean seed from this bag and plant it in a little pot. Then we'll watch and see what happens."

Nadine hands out small pots made out of thin cardboard, and Tino gets to carry the paper bag full of seeds around the classroom for everyone to take one. I reach my hand into the bag and feel the smooth beans. When I pull my hand out, I look down at my seed and am surprised to see that it looks like a kidney bean. It is red and shaped like an oval. It reminds me of the kidney beans they have in the salad bar at school sometimes, except this one is as hard as a rock.

I write my name on the flimsy pot and fill it with soft, brown dirt. I push the bean down into the soil and sprinkle water on top. After that, everyone lines up their pots along the shelf by the window so they can get some sun and start to grow.

* * *

To my surprise, when school is over, it's Daddy who

picks me up.

"Daddy!" I shout and jump into his arms.

He's wearing his work clothes—a short-sleeved work shirt and pants. His eyes have tired little creases around them, but a smile fills his whole face.

"Why are you picking me up? Where's Papa?"

"Papa's at home. I finished work early and wanted to spend the afternoon with you today. The big project I've been working on is done, so I finally get a break from the early mornings and late nights at work," he explains with a grin on his face. "Want to go to Waneka Lake?"

"Yes, yes, yes! May Nadine and Emery come?" I bounce right out of his arms and twirl in a circle around him.

"Sure, let's go ask their parents."

* * *

A little while later, we're all at Waneka Lake with our pants rolled up and toes in the sand. In early March, you never know what kind of day you're going to get in Colorado. Sometimes it can be warm and feel like a shorts and T-shirt day. But other days, it can snow as much as it did in winter.

Daddy sits back and chats with Emery's dad while Emery, Nadine, and I write our names in the sand with sticks. Even though the air is warm, when the water splashes on our feet, it feels like ice so we prance in and out of the lake, whooping and hollering.

We climb in the trees bordering the lake and walk as

far as we can balance on the long tree branches that bend down to the shore. Then we play a game of tag that ends at the playground. I race to the top of the slide, shout "I'm the queen of the castle!" then zip down the slide.

Emery runs over to the bike path and exclaims, "Guys, look! It's a turtle!"

Nadine and I race over and sure enough, there's a big turtle walking along the trail by the lake. We bend down and watch it plod slowly away from the path toward the playground.

"Daddy!" I shout. "There's a turtle! May we pick him up? I want to take him to the lake. He's going to get squished over here."

Daddy jogs over and says, "Wow, look at him! Yes, Sophie, you may carefully pick him up to get him over to the lake. Put him down somewhere a little less crowded."

I reach down and pick him up as gently as I can. I wrap my hands around his smooth, hard shell. He's so big that my fingers don't even touch in the middle. As soon as he's in the air, his legs wiggle wildly, searching for the ground.

Nadine points to some bushes and declares, "He'll be safe over there."

I carry him as carefully as I can. I kneel down next to the bushes and hand him to Emery, who holds him for a moment, then passes him to Nadine. We all pet him gently, then Nadine lowers him to the ground and lets go.

"Let's name him Yellow," Emery suggests.

"That's an interesting name," Emery's dad says.

"It's because he has a yellow stripe around his shell,"

Emery explains.

"Oh, look at that," Daddy says. "So he does."

We agree it's a great name and watch Yellow toddle slowly toward a clump of grass and take a big bite. He stays there, chewing thoughtfully, obviously not too concerned about getting away from us quickly.

"Well, we should get going, kids," Daddy states. "It's going to start cooling down soon and we've got to head home to make dinner."

We say our goodbyes, stroking Yellow's smooth shell one more time, and leave.

* * *

For the rest of the week, the weather stays warm. Daddy is at home later in the mornings and earlier in the afternoons. But the following week after school, I'm playing in my bedroom when I hear Daddy and Papa talking in loud voices downstairs. Daddy is upset. I can tell by the way his words are clipped short at the end of his sentences.

I put down the blocks I was building with and creep to the stairs to listen. Their voices are muffled, so I quietly step down the stairs and into the hallway.

Papa murmurs something in a low voice and I hold still, watching them in the kitchen. I don't know why Daddy's angry, but I try not to breathe. He moves like a big storm cloud, like he could explode at any moment. A tight ball clenches in the pit of my stomach, making me feel uneasy.

Then his voice gets really loud and he shouts, "I can't believe it! We already discussed this less than a month ago! But now she's apparently forgotten all of the hours that I put in and doesn't care that she promised I could work less this month!" Without taking a breath, Daddy slams a cupboard door closed with a loud bang and shouts, "I am *not* a robot!"

The sound makes me jump, but I don't move any closer to them. Then Daddy turns and sees me standing there. He takes a slow, deep breath and asks, "Did you hear me yelling, Sophie?"

I nod quietly, but don't say anything.

"I'm sorry if I scared you. I'm just upset because my boss wants me to work extra hours again, like I've been doing for the past few months. But she was supposed to let me work less now that my big project is done and the new programmer is trained." He takes another deep breath, pulls a chair out from the table, and slumps down heavily.

I walk over and climb onto his lap. Then I lean my head against his chest and listen to his heart beat *thump, thump, thump.* I breathe in his comforting smell, like the woods and cinnamon, and my stomach starts to relax. "And now she wants you to work more again?"

Daddy sighs and strokes my hair. "Yeah. I know it's been hard on you to have me work so much lately, and honestly, it's also been too much for me. I talked to my boss about it a while ago and we agreed that I would get some hard-earned time off as soon as I trained our newest team member."

I look up at him. He puts his arms around me and I breathe deeply again.

He speaks slower and takes even breaths now that I am sitting on his lap. "I pushed through all those long hours because I knew that a nice break was coming up. And now that it's time for my break, she doesn't want me to take it. She just got another big client and she wants me to take the lead on this, which would mean even more hours."

For the first time since I've come in, Papa chimes in. "Daddy and I were talking it over and he's going to set up a meeting with his boss. One thing we're thinking about is Daddy taking a week off for spring break and then going back part-time."

I sit up straighter then and a smile breaks out across my face like sunshine. "Yes, yes, yes! Oh please, Daddy! Then we will have enough time to take care of Spot!"

I expect Daddy to grumble and say no, but instead he chuckles. "Leave it to you, Sophie, to put things into perspective for us."

* * *

The next day at school, Colby says it's time to continue our experiment. "Now we're going to make observations. Use all of your senses. You probably won't taste or hear much, but what do you see, smell, or feel?"

I look down at my notebook. Observation: I'm hungry. No, that's not about the plant. Observation: It's cold outside. That was better, but still not entirely about the plant. Observation: My seed has sprouted.

A couple of pots still have only dirt, but a lot of our seeds have started to sprout. Short stems have poked their heads above the soil. A few more have even started to unfurl tender, light green leaves.

I look around the classroom and nearly everyone is finishing up their observations of the plant. I look back at my paper and decide to add another sentence. Observation: The soil is wet. I think this is important because water is one of the most important things a plant needs to grow.

We turn in our observations to Colby. He hangs up a big poster paper with a picture of a bean plant and a bunch of blank lines at the bottom. Emery raises his hand to volunteer to write all of our observations on the poster, and Tino gets to read what everyone has written.

* * *

Papa picks me up after school and I worry that Daddy will still be at work. That he'll have to keep working too much and he'll be grumpy all the time.

But when we get home, Daddy is already there. He has an apron tied around his waist, a spatula in one hand, and a deep smile across his face. Sometimes when he smiles, it only reaches his lips. This time, the smile goes right up across his cheeks and into his eyes, making them sparkle. There are still small creases at the corners of his eyes, but they are harder to see through his sparkling smile.

"Daddy!" I shout and jump into his arms. "You're home! What are you cooking?"

The kitchen smells amazing and all of a sudden, I feel

like I haven't eaten in days.

"Here. Sit, sit, Sophie," he says and pulls a chair out for me with a flourish.

I sit down and eagerly look around the kitchen. He spoons tabouli salad into a small bowl, then drizzles extra lemon on top. As I eat, I look around to see what else he is making. There are vegetable peels, flour, and dirty dishes spread all over the counter.

"The rest is for dinner, but try a bite of this," Daddy says and leans over with a spoonful of cinnamon-spiced sweet potatoes.

I chew and my mouth is filled with an explosion of cinnamon and ginger. "Yum!" I say with my mouth full. This is what is making our house smell so wonderful. The aroma reminds me of Thanksgiving. I love it.

"Okay, okay, one more thing to try," Daddy declares and gives me another bite of a curry dumpling. It fills me with a delightful warmth as I eat it, and I smile up at him.

I love when Daddy cooks. The kitchen seems brighter and warmer. He turns music on loud and dances around the kitchen, stirring up puffs of flour and swirls of seasonings until it seems like the bowls themselves are going to hop up and dance with him. When he really gets into it, some of the food goes flying and the counters are speckled with dried bits of dough and mashed up bits of vegetables. Even the fruit in our fruit bowl sitting on the counter gets covered with flour.

Lately, he's been so busy that he hasn't had time to cook, so our countertops have been plainly clean and our kitchen quieter. Today, though, he must be making up for lost time.

"Good news, Sophie. I met with my boss again today and told her that I can't keep working such crazy hours. That, in fact, I need to reduce my hours. You know we've been wanting to do that for a while now, and Papa and I looked at our budget and realized that I only need to work part-time. After a little convincing, my boss agreed. So I'll be able to stay home with you over spring break next week and only work part-time after that!" Daddy tells me and smiles.

"Yes!" I shout and jump off my chair. Daddy takes my hand, spins me in a circle, then dips me back. I lift one leg up like a ballerina and bend down backward as far as I can. Then he pulls me up, whirls around, and pulls Papa up from his chair, dragging him into the kitchen as well. We all dance like that for what feels like hours, while the loud, happy music and the smell of cinnamon, ginger, and curry swirl around us in a big, delicious cloud.

Chapter 13

When I see Spot that Saturday, I can tell he's been lonely. He's lying in a dog bed, head on his paws, with a sad look on his face. He watches the other dogs play, but doesn't join in. As soon as he sees me, he jumps up and bounds over to me, only to stop midway and race back to the doggie toy box for his favorite ball, then gallop back even faster. I laugh and reach down to scratch his neck, paying extra attention to rub behind his ears the way he loves.

"Hey, Spot. I missed you. Looks like you feel the same way."

He leans into me, asking me to pet him and throw the ball both at once. "I can't pet you while you're chasing your ball, you silly pup," I say, shaking my head. I quickly give him a pet on the head, then stroke all the way down his back to his wagging tail. He looks up at me with those kind, brown eyes and his face lights up with a smile again.

We trot outside to the play area and I reach back to throw the ball as hard as I can, but it slips behind me. Instead of going forward, it falls behind my back. As my arm flies forward, Spot tears across the grass in search of the ball that didn't get thrown. I spin around to grab it as he looks back at me quizzically. I throw it again, and this time it actually goes forward. Spot races after it, all thought focused on grabbing that ball.

I hear laughter and turn to see Hayes jogging over to

me. "That was hilarious!" he says, cracking up.

We play like that for a while, taking turns throwing the ball back and forth. As I watch Spot race from one end of the field and back, part of me hopes that he will be adopted soon so he's not lonely anymore. But another, deeper part of me wishes fiercely that he will just hang on a little longer until we can take him home. Now that Daddy will only work part-time, shouldn't we have enough time to take care of Spot soon?

* * *

The next week is spring break. Nadine is on vacation with her family, so we're taking care of their dogs. Today Emery is at my house for a playdate and Daddy takes us over to Nadine's house to get the dogs for a walk.

We each take hold of a leash and walk toward the creek. It snowed an inch or two over the night, and as we walk across the white ground, our feet leave muddy, brown tracks behind us. This is a spring snow, not the light, fluffy kind we get in the middle of winter. It's the heavy, wet kind of snow that weighs down tree branches full of new green shoots and flower blossoms. The kind that starts melting as soon as it hits the ground. As we walk along the creek path, snow falls off the trees in giant plops that leave icy trails down my neck. I shiver and snug my hood up over my head.

Emery happily skips along beside us. "Look, Sophie, I'm a deer!"

I look up and smile. Emery is indeed trotting around

like a happy deer, or maybe more like a fawn with its awkward gait and unsteady legs. Luna is trotting along beside him. I laugh the way I always do when I play with Emery.

"Watch me, Emery! I'm a duck!" I point my heels together and waddle slowly side to side. When I look back at the trail, the tracks I've left in the snow have changed. They're closer together now and blur together in the shape of a *V*.

We follow Daddy as he turns off the main trail and starts walking down a smaller path closer to the creek. Emery hops up on a fallen down log and tries to balance, but slides down one side. He grabs onto a small branch to steady himself and a mound of snow plops down from the tree onto his head. "Eee! That's cold!" he shouts, shaking it off.

When we reach the creek, Emery and I toss rocks into the water. They plop as they sink into the dark water, leaving waves rippling out in circles. Daddy hands us flat ones that are smooth on one side, but Daddy is the only one who can make them skip across the surface of the water.

* * *

Over the next few days, I watch Daddy and Papa. They both seem to be relaxing more. With Daddy home for the week, he's not rushing off to work. Instead, he sits with Papa in the mornings, drinking tea and chatting or reading. I see more smiles between them and hear more laughter than I have in a long time.

Mostly, though, I watch Daddy. I can tell that something is going on inside of him. First, I notice that his eyebrows aren't scrunched up at the top of his forehead anymore. His eyes seem kinder too. And he hums to himself as he cleans the kitchen.

But in the afternoons, I see him pacing around the house, like he's looking for something. Only I don't think he even knows what he's looking for. He straightens the books on the coffee table, wipes down the counters, and looks at his phone. Papa is at work so there's no easy laughter and tea.

"What are you doing, Daddy?" I ask.

Daddy looks up and sighs. "I know it's silly, but I'm not used to all of this free time yet." He chuckles. "I don't know what to do with myself."

"We could play Chutes and Ladders," I suggest.

Daddy smiles, then nods. "Sure, Sophie. That would be nice."

When we sit down and play, I can tell that he is still pacing in his mind, because his eyes have that faraway look like the sky on a gray, cloudy day.

* * *

When I go back to school after spring break, I'm shocked to see our plants in the window. They have grown a ton while we've been gone! All of the beans in the little pots have sprouted and the tender green shoots have darkened into thick, dark green leaves.

Colby points to the paper with our observations on it. "Okay, let's go through these one by one, and then we'll do our final steps of the scientific method—analysis and conclusion. Who would like to read?"

Tino shoots his hand up in the air and Colby nods. "Okay, the first guess . . . er, hypothesis was that the seeds will grow leaves that are the same color."

My head perks up. That was my guess.

"Great, Tino, thank you," Colby says, and his eyes light up. "Now is the really fun part. Let's go over and take a look."

We crowd around the windowsill, craning our necks to see all of the little plants.

"Most of the leaves are dark green now," I declare, looking over the bunch.

"Except that one has a little bit of yellow around the edges," Nadine adds, pointing to one plant off to the side and sliding it closer to the window. "Aww, man, that one's mine too."

"Interesting," Colby says. "Why do you think that happened?"

"I don't know," Nadine answers, thinking. "I made sure to water it every time we came in from recess and got back from lunch and in the morning."

"Hmm . . . I see," Colby says, nodding his head. "Did you also water it when the rest of the class watered their plants during science time?"

Nadine nods and realization dawns on her face. "Oh . . . maybe I watered it too much?"

Colby nods and pats her shoulder. "It sounds like it. I know you were trying to give it all the water it needed, but sometimes too much water can actually hurt the plant too. Okay, so we learned that most of the leaves were the same dark green color except ones that got too much water and turned yellow."

Colby hangs another piece of poster paper up and Emery writes down our conclusion, "Same color leaves unless too much water."

Next Tino reads, "Okay, the next hypothesis was that some plants will have more leaves than others."

We turn back to the windowsill and quickly begin counting the leaves on each plant. Most of them only have two leaves, but some are starting to grow more.

"Cool, so it looks like the plants all started out with two leaves and some are now growing more," Colby sums up as Emery jots down our conclusion.

We continue analyzing our hypotheses and coming up with conclusions. Finally, we reach Emery's guess that some plants wouldn't grow at all.

"I guess I was wrong," Emery says in a dejected voice.

"That's okay," Colby tells him. "It's never a bad thing to make guesses about what might happen. Sometimes you guess right and sometimes you don't. The important thing is that you're learning every time you use the scientific method."

* * *

The next Thursday is my adoptive birthday. That

evening, Papa gets out the scrapbook we've made of our family and we all snuggle up on the couch together.

The first few pages are filled with photos and tales about Daddy and Papa. There's a photo of Papa as a baby taking a bath in the kitchen sink. Gramps is holding him up with one hand and lathering bubbles on his head with the other. There's a photo of Daddy riding a bright red tricycle and smiling into the camera. Then there are photos of Daddy and Papa in college and on their wedding day.

Each page is filled with photographs and handwritten stories. Some are funny stories about silly things they did when they were young. Others are sweet stories, like how Daddy knew that Papa was the one.

After I was born, the pages start to fill up with pictures and stories about me. There's a photo of my birth mom holding me in the hospital where I was born. My birth dad is leaning toward us, peering at the bundle in her arms. There are two handwritten letters taped to the same page. I know what they say without reading them.

One is from my birth mom about how she knew she was too young to raise a child, and she hoped that I could have a better life. The other is from my birth dad about how hard it was to let me go, and how they tried to raise me, but after a few weeks, they both knew that I deserved better than they could give me.

I flip to the last page. There's a picture of me on the swings at school in second grade, and another of me playing at Waneka Lake. I read what Daddy wrote about me being in the spelling bee last year. Then I turn the page and read what Papa wrote about how much he loved to read with me, and how happy he was to see me fall in love with reading on my own.

When I look at my handwriting from last year, I think it looks like a baby's handwriting. I wrote about going to Seattle and watching the fish throwers throw big, slimy fish to each other at Pike Place Market. It was so loud and exciting.

"Man, remember how much fun that was?" Daddy says with a smile.

Papa nods and turns the page. He pulls out a blank sheet of paper from the scrapbook and turns to me. "Would you like to go first?"

I take the paper and start writing about my favorite things that have happened over the last year. I write about how glad I was that Nadine was in my class this year, and how much I loved doing math with Maddie, the math dog, and best of all, getting to volunteer at the shelter and meet Spot.

When I'm done, Papa takes the paper and flips it over. Then he writes on the back about how much he loved making my Halloween costume this year, and how special it was having everyone over for Thanksgiving. Daddy writes about how much he loved spending time with me at Waneka Lake and how he hopes to spend more time together this year.

Afterward, Papa hands me a box of stationery. I like the one that has a picture of a dog who stepped in an ink bottle, leaving a trail of paw prints across the page. I write a short note to both of my birth parents. I tell them what my life is like and my favorite things, and how I really hope I can get a dog this year. Then I help Daddy choose a photo of me to send to them.

That night, the three of us have a special dinner together. We tell stories and crack each other up with funny jokes. After dinner, I am a good clean-up helper and place everyone's dishes on the counter.

Daddy comments to Papa, "She really has grown up, hasn't she?"

* * *

One night a few weeks later, I'm reading a book on the couch. *Otis* from the Kitty Corner series. Papa sits down next to me and Daddy snuggles in from my other side. I look up. A twinkling in their eyes makes me immediately put my book down.

"Sophie?" Papa asks.

"Yeah?" I respond, wondering where this is going.

"Daddy and I wanted to give you a belated birthday present," he begins.

"We've noticed that you've been really grown-up lately," Daddy adds. "And we finally have more time to take care of a dog, so we wanted to know if you still want a dog? Do you still want to adopt Spot?"

For a moment, time stands still. It feels like a hundred thoughts explode inside of my head at once, then tumble out one after the other, the way I do when I'm running too fast and can't get my feet underneath me. I have waited so long for this moment; I can't believe it's actually happening! Spot! I see his face in my mind and my heart explodes with joy! My thoughts whirl this way and that, all clamoring to be the first thought out of my mouth.

"Yes!" My book tumbles out of my lap and I don't even bother to put the bookmark in. "Really? I knew it! I *knew* it! Oh, I can't believe it! When can we get him? Can we go right now? I'll get my jacket."

I jump up and am halfway to the hall before Daddy and Papa can even get a word in.

Daddy chuckles and Papa says, "I told you she'd say yes." As though there were any doubt what my answer would be.

I shrug my arms through my sleeves, but Papa motions me over onto his lap. "Adoption hours are over and the shelter is closing soon, darling. We'll sleep on it and go first thing in the morning."

I stand there with one arm in my jacket and one arm out, the other sleeve hanging down limply at my side. I don't want to go tomorrow. I don't want to wait another minute. What if they change their mind overnight?

Daddy steps in. "It's okay, sweetie. No one else is going to take Spot before we get there. But if it makes you feel better, we can call them right now and let them know that we'll be in tomorrow to adopt him."

I nod. "Yes, please. Oh, I wish Spot could answer the phone. Can you tell them to tell Spot tonight? I don't want him to spend another lonely night thinking no one is ever going to adopt him. I know he'll understand if they tell him."

Daddy agrees and pulls out his phone. I watch as he dials, then puts the phone on speaker so we all can hear.

"Thank you for calling Lucky Dog Animal Shelter, this is Liam," a voice on the other end answers. I've never met Liam. I shift from one foot to the other.

"Hello, this is Samuel Granbould. I'm calling because we'd like to come by tomorrow to adopt one of your dogs, Spot," Daddy explains.

"Oh, that's wonderful!" Liam exclaims. "He's been wanting a forever home for some time now. I'll make a note that you'd like to adopt him. We're closing up now, but we open for adoptions at nine o'clock tomorrow morning."

"Nine o'clock sounds great. I don't think our daughter will let us come a minute later than that," Daddy states with a smile.

"Perfect, we'll have everything ready for you in the morning." Liam sounds like he's about to hang up.

I tap Daddy's arm and whisper, "Tell him to tell Spot."

"Oh, and one more thing," Daddy says. "We would really love it if you could tell Spot tonight that he'll be adopted tomorrow. Our daughter would really appreciate it. She has quite a bond with him."

"Yes, of course. I understand. Tell your daughter that I believe that even though dogs don't speak our same language, I'm sure he'll be able to understand," Liam reassures us. "And in a few hours, she'll be able to see him and tell him herself."

"Great, thank you again," Daddy says and hangs up.

I am still standing there with one arm in my jacket. Daddy stands up and helps me tug it gently off my shoulder, then hangs it up in the hallway.

"We need to go shopping!" I exclaim, thinking about everything we'll need for Spot when he gets here tomorrow. *Tomorrow!*

"We can stop at the store first thing in the morning, but right now, sweetie, it's time to head upstairs for bed," Daddy declares.

My mind is racing and there are so many things I want to do besides sleep, but I follow him upstairs anyway.

"He absolutely needs a collar, and a leash. And food. Oh my gosh, we're going to have to get him a food bowl, unless you think he'll use one of ours?" I pause on the stairs and look up questioningly at Daddy.

"We'll be sure to get him his own special dog dish, food, and water," he states.

"Okay, good. Then we'll have to make sure he has toys, and his favorite ball. And a nice, comfy place to sleep. Can he sleep on my bed? He can snuggle on my soft blanket," I say as we walk into my bedroom.

Daddy nods, then motions me over to sit next to him on my love seat.

"Don't worry, Sophie. We'll make sure Spot gets everything he needs to feel comfortable."

As he picks up a book to read, I snuggle in close and listen. At first, I'm so excited that I'm too distracted to listen. I can't stop thinking about everything we'll need, and how wonderful it will be to finally have Spot in my own home. But soon, the story calms me down and lulls me into a sleepy state and I start to yawn. When the chapter is over, Daddy tells me to get up, brush my teeth, and get ready for bed.

When I climb into bed, I lie under my blanket quietly for a long time, picturing Spot curled up on my feet. One more night. That's all I have to wait, just one more night. I think of Spot curled up at the animal shelter and hope that he knows that's all he has to wait too.

Chapter 14

As soon as my eyes start to open, I am moving, jumping out of bed. I startle Orion, who grumpily moves to the side and stretches. His growl turns into a yawn so wide I can see his teeth and the roof of his mouth. I reach over and scratch him behind the ears. He stretches so hard that his whole body shakes, then he turns in a small circle and plops back down.

I pull my clothes on faster than lightning, sprint downstairs, and grab a banana. I am pulling the milk from the fridge when Daddy staggers in, blinking.

"Sophie, what are you doing up so early? It's only five thirty," he says and yawns.

Papa stumbles in behind him and declares, "Well, it looks like it's time to start the day. We only have three and a half hours until adoptions open."

Daddy tries to suppress a smirk, but his face is overcome with a yawn instead. "Yeah, no going back from here. I'll go shower."

Papa makes tea, and I finish my banana and take a big gulp of my milk. Then I get to work. By six thirty, I have brushed my teeth, combed my hair, found an extra blanket for Spot, laid it out on my bed, made a list of everything that we'll need to get at the store, and I'm ready to walk out the door.

"Is it time?" I eagerly shout upstairs to Papa and Daddy.

They don't respond.

"Is it time?" I shout even louder without putting my pencil down.

"Not yet, Sophie," I hear Daddy shout back.

I put my pencil down and bound up the stairs. "What are you doing? How much longer?"

Daddy is brushing his teeth and Papa is in the shower.

"We aren't leaving for an hour, Sophie. Why don't you go make a welcome home picture for Spot while you wait?" Daddy answers.

I want to go now. But I turn around and stomp down the stairs one step at a time, making sure that Daddy hears each loud *thump* on every stair.

I sit down at the kitchen table and color a picture for Spot. I draw our whole family: Daddy, Papa, me, Artemis, Orion, and Spot. *Spot!* A smile flashes across my face thinking about him becoming part of our family. Then I add "Welcome Home!!" in big letters across the top of the page, and add a bright red heart on each side. I get tape out of the drawer and hang Spot's welcome home sign on our front door.

Daddy and Papa start preparing the cats for our new family member. The first thing they do is put the cats' water dish in their bedroom. Then Papa scoops some food into their food dish and sets it next to the water.

"Why are you putting that in here?" I ask. I'm sitting on the floor in their bedroom, petting Artemis while Orion sleeps on the bed, curled into a ball.

"We'll keep them in here with the door closed at first.

It's a big deal bringing home a new pet, so we want to make sure that Artemis and Orion have a safe space they can stay in while they get used to having Spot around," Papa explains as he lugs in the kitty litter box.

Daddy adds, "Plus, Spot is a lot bigger than they are, so they might be a little bit scared at first. We'll just go slow until they're comfortable enough to wander around the house together. But until then, we're going to keep them separated so we can keep an eye on them."

"It may be a little while before they're ready to see each other," Papa declares. "Animals use their sense of smell much more than we do, so we'll introduce their smell to each other first. We'll bring the blanket they usually sleep on with us so Spot can get used to their smell on the way home."

I stroke Artemis one more time, then shine a laser light around the room for her to chase. Finally, they say it's time to leave, so I grab my list and skip out to the car.

* * *

After stopping at the store and buying dog food, dog dishes, doggie bags, Spot's favorite treats, a few toys, a leash, identification tags, and a safety harness for the car, we pull into the nearly empty parking lot of the animal shelter and I jump out of the car as quickly as I can. It is only 8:49 a.m., so we wait by the front door for a few minutes before Jazmin appears and unlocks the door with a click.

"Good morning!" she says cheerfully. "My name is

Jazmin. You must be Sophie's dad, Samuel."

"Good morning," Daddy replies, reaching out to shake her hand. "I think we met briefly when we volunteered over Thanksgiving weekend. And, of course, you know Sophie and Augustus."

"Ah yes, good to see you again," Jazmin says, taking his hand. Then she turns to me and Papa and says, "And how are you two? I heard that you're here to adopt Spot today. Right this way, follow me."

Jazmin turns left and leads us down a hallway I don't recognize. I watch her curly, brown hair bounce up and down on her shoulders as we speed down the hallway. I am so full of excitement today that I'm going so fast that I almost step on the back of her shoes when she stops.

Jazmin just flashes me one of her big smiles and opens the door, ushering us into a small office filled with filing cabinets and overgrown plants.

"We have a little bit of paperwork for you to fill out before you take Spot home this morning," she explains.

I sit on a hard wood chair and swing my legs back and forth. As the adults discuss the papers on the desk in front of them, I look around the room. A bright green plant with big leaves sits on top of a filing cabinet. Its vines are pinned to the wall and climb all the way to the ceiling, making the room look like a beautiful jungle.

"Because Spot has been here a while, he's up to date on all of his vaccinations. He is an older dog, but his health is good enough that he can leave today without any procedures," Jazmin explains. "Our vet tech is doing a final exit exam, of course, to give him one last check over and let you know if there's anything you may need to follow up on."

Daddy and Papa nod as she talks.

I tug on Daddy's sleeve. "Spot's okay, though, right?"

"Please don't tug—" Daddy starts to say.

But Jazmin jumps in. "Yes, Spot is just fine. But even though this is a wonderful day for him, it is a very big change and he may need some time to adjust." She turns back to Daddy and Papa. "And, of course, if you need anything or have any questions, you can always give us a call."

"Thank you," Papa says.

Jazmin smiles her bright, cheerful smile and stands up.

"Here's your welcome bag with a few comfort items to take home for Spot," she says with a smile, handing Papa a small paper bag with twine handles.

I reach over and pull it toward me so fast that one of the handles rips off one side.

Daddy looks down and furrows his eyebrows.

Papa hands it to me and says, "Here you go, Sophie. Would you hold onto this for us?"

I nod and grasp the bag to look inside. I see Spot's favorite ball that we always play with—a worn tennis ball that is fraying around the edges. I shove some papers to the side and see the dog treats that he loves.

"Thank you, again, very much," Daddy is saying.

Papa nods and I break into a wide grin. At last, it's time to get Spot and bring him home. We follow Jazmin into another part of the shelter I've never been in and turn right at the end of a long hall. This time, I'm practically running and wind up in front of everyone.

Jazmin cautions me, "Slow down a bit there, Sophie. You never know when someone is going to come flying around a corner."

I try to slow down, but I keep picturing Spot. I just want to see him and throw my arms around him right this minute!

"This is the medical wing of the animal shelter," Jazmin explains, pausing at the last room to hold the door open for us. "Here you go, right this way."

We enter the room and see Spot sitting on a low table with a soft fabric covering. A man with a stethoscope is kneeling down beside him, petting him gently and murmuring to him quietly.

"Good morning," he says, looking up with a smile.

The man starts to introduce himself, but as soon as Spot sees me, he leaps up and bounds right off the little table. He shouts a few happy barks, then runs around me in circles and nuzzles his nose into my hand.

"Oh, Spot!" I say and bend down to pet him. "Spot, it's your adoption day! We're taking you home today. Would you like that? Do you want to come home with us?"

Spot must know that this is a special day, because he yips again and wags his tail harder than I've ever seen. He has so much energy that it's hard to remember that we were concerned about the way he moped around gloomily before. I'm trying to hug him and scratch behind his ears the way I know he likes, but Spot is too excited. He prances all around the room from Daddy to Papa to Jazmin and back to the vet, whose name I still haven't heard, and back to me, then he starts all over again. Everyone is beaming.

The vet chuckles and says, "We were just finishing up. Spot has a clean bill of health and, as you can see, he is ready to move on."

Papa pulls a small silver circle with our phone number on it out of his pocket and gently convinces Spot to sit still while he attaches it to his collar. When he steps back, it jingles against Spot's name tag and vaccine tags. It sounds like little bells chiming. It is music to my ears.

Daddy fastens the leash to his collar.

"I want to hold it!" I cry, grabbing the leash from Daddy's hands.

"Don't forget to say 'please.' There's no rush," Daddy reminds me.

"Sorry, Daddy. Please," I say.

We leave the exam room with Spot happily trotting along beside us. This time, we curve back around and pass the main dog area.

"May we stop to say goodbye?" I ask, then add, "Please?"

Daddy nods and Jazmin says, "That would be nice, Sophie."

When we open the door, I can see other staff members playing with the dogs inside. I recognize some of them from the pictures hanging on the wall. Spot pulls me across the room and rubs his nose right into an elderly woman's

143

hand. She looks down and smiles.

"Look who's going to a new home today!" she exclaims, gently stroking the top of Spot's head all the way down his back. His brown fur ruffles in waves under her hands.

Spot gives one happy little bark, then leans into Jazmin. As Jazmin bends down to pet the scruff of his neck, Spot turns and does something I've never seen him do. He spins around quickly in a circle and tries to chase his tail.

"Oh man," Jazmin declares, "I've seen Spot light up when you're around, Sophie, but I haven't seen him this excited in a long time."

I unhook his leash and watch as Spot races around the room, making happy little yipping noises as he passes the other dogs. A few times he stops and sniffs another dog and jumps around before racing on to the next one.

When all of our goodbyes have been said, we hook Spot's leash back on and walk down the hall.

"Are you sure his leash is on okay, Daddy?" I ask as we open the door.

Daddy checks it and nods. "It's great."

Spot follows us out the door and to our car. Daddy puts on Spot's safety harness and buckles him into the seat next to me. Papa hands him the cats' blanket. Spot's nose twitches furiously back and forth as he takes in all of the new smells around him. I reach over from my seat and lay my hand on his back. Spot moves his paws forward and lays his head down, looking up at me with his radiant eyes.

I close my eyes for a moment and let it soak in. Today is the day. We are finally bringing Spot home to be part of our family. Peace settles over me and I rest my head and relax.

* * *

I must have fallen asleep, because when I open my eyes, Papa is opening the door and unbuckling Spot. I yawn and look around with bleary eyes. Spot hops up, full of energy again. When we get out of the car, Spot tilts his head and looks up at me, as if wondering where we are.

"We're here, Spot," I tell him. "This is your new home."

As soon as we get inside, Spot starts sniffing all over the place. Daddy unhooks his leash and hangs it on a hook by the door, and we follow Spot from room to room as he explores our house.

Papa sets the gift bag down on the coffee table in the living room, and I pull out Spot's ball. He licks it happily, but continues roaming around the house, smelling everything. When he gets upstairs, Spot lingers outside of Daddy and Papa's room. He sticks his nose near the gap under the door and paws at the floor.

I hear a meow come from inside. There is one second of silence, then Spot leaps up and barks loudly. A loud hiss and a growl escape from inside the room and Spot barks again. Daddy grabs onto Spot's collar and gently tugs him down the hall into my bedroom. Meanwhile, Papa quietly opens the door and slips inside his bedroom to comfort the cats. He carries in the blanket that Spot laid on in the car.

"Look, Spot, here's where you'll sleep tonight," I say, patting my bed. "Want to jump up, buddy?"

But Spot is whining, looking behind him down the hall toward the bedroom with our cats inside. I kneel down and pet him, but Spot continues to whine, picking one paw up after another, over and over, as though he were stepping in place.

"It's okay, Spot. They're family," I say soothingly. "You'll get used to them."

But Spot doesn't get used to them. He starts to bark again.

"I think he's had enough of an introduction for the first time," Daddy says. "Let's take him outside for a little walk."

Daddy hollers to Papa through their bedroom door as we walk by, "We're going for a little walk. Be back soon."

Then he grabs Spot's leash and we head outside. Spot romps around happily, checking out clumps of grass here and sticks there. He isn't growling anymore and is back to his normal, happy self.

Looking around at my neighborhood, holding the end of Spot's leash, I feel complete. I am bursting with excitement and everything seems brighter. It is mid-morning and the sun is shining brightly now with the strong light of late spring.

Spot jogs happily beside me toward our trail, busily stopping to sniff at flowers, grass, fence posts, and trees. The air is warm and filled with a feeling of good things coming true. I couldn't have wiped the huge smile from my face if someone had told me to.

When Spot stops to poop, I look up at Daddy.

"You can do it," he tells me encouragingly. "Put the bag over your hand like this, pick it up, and pull the bag inside out over your hand."

"Maybe you should show me first," I say.

"You got this," he answers, taking the leash from me.

I nod and look down at the brown pile. It stinks and makes me want to gag. I put the bag over my hand like Daddy showed me. Then I turn away, take a big breath, and plug my nose with my other hand. Then I quickly turn back, reach down, and pick it up. I pull the bag inside out as fast as I can, but it still smells awful. I look back at the ground. Half of the pile is still there. I set the first bag to the side and repeat the steps, making sure to take a big breath and plug my nose beforehand again.

I let Daddy hold Spot's leash while we walk down the trail toward the garbage can. As soon as I throw the bags away, Daddy hands the leash back to me.

"Good job, Sophie," Daddy praises me. "You really must love him to be so willing to help clean up his messes."

"I know, Daddy. I love him so much," I respond, beaming. I would do anything for Spot.

* * *

When we get back home, Papa greets us at the door, but the cats are still in the bedroom. Right away, Spot's nose begins twitching furiously again. We lead him over to the kitchen where Papa has laid out his food and water dishes.

"Here you go," Papa says soothingly. "Are you hungry?" Before Papa has barely even finished the question, Spot dives in and devours the food with large gulps.

Daddy laughs and says, "Well, that answers that. Seems like he worked up an appetite. Speaking of appetites, who's hungry for lunch?"

Suddenly, I realize my stomach is growling. "I'm starving!" I tell him.

Spot and I play tug with his new chew toy in the living room while Daddy makes lunch. The rest of the afternoon flies by in a swirl of walks, playtime, and rest. Just before dinner, I ask to check on Artemis and Orion. Daddy and Papa agree to keep an eye on Spot while I sneak upstairs.

When I open the bedroom door, Artemis is curled up on the bed and Orion is sitting in the windowsill. I close the door quickly as they scurry over, winding themselves between my legs and purring loudly.

"Hey, guys," I murmur, sitting down on the floor to pet them. "Wait until you meet Spot. Well, I know you heard him through the door and can smell his scent on the blanket Papa brought you, but I mean just wait until you've really met him. You're going to love him!"

I stay there, quietly scratching behind their ears and stroking their heads all the way down their backs. Artemis tires of my pets and wanders over to her water dish. Then Orion stalks a few feet away and lies down on the floor. I listen to Orion purring contentedly for a few minutes before heading back downstairs, feeling elated.

When it's time for bed, however, my elation fades. I try to take Spot down the hall toward my room, but he refuses to walk past Daddy and Papa's room. He paws frantically at the floor, then leans down low and sticks his nose near the bottom of the door. The more Spot whines and barks, the more Artemis and Orion hiss and growl from the other side of the door.

Finally, Daddy picks Spot up and carries him into my room. Papa and I follow, and Papa shuts the door behind us.

"I think it's best if we leave your bedroom door closed tonight, Sophie," Daddy decides as he sets Spot down.

"Why are Spot and the cats acting so mean to each other?" I ask worriedly.

Spot sniffs around my room, then hops up on my bed and rolls on his back.

"Well, like they said at the shelter, it's a really big change for both the cats and for Spot," Papa explains gently. "They don't know each other yet and because there's a lot of unknowns, it can be really scary for them."

I nod, thinking about how scary it was starting the winter break camp when I didn't know what it would be like. "How long will it take for them to get used to each other?" I ask.

"Hopefully not long. Probably a few days at least, but we'll just play it by ear and introduce them little bit by little bit," Papa states.

"Oh, Spot," I say, rubbing his tummy. "You've got to be nice to Artemis and Orion. They're nothing to be afraid of."

I yawn and Spot rolls over to his side. I fall asleep quickly with Spot sleeping contentedly at the foot of my bed.

Chapter 15

It is dark and I'm dreaming that Spot and I are racing down a trail. Except the trail is made up of clouds. We hop easily from one fluffy, white cloud to another, feeling the weight of our footsteps press down on the springy clouds. The clouds darken and a storm begins. The thunder starts to shake the clouds, making me wobble and lose my balance.

As the thunder crashes again, louder this time, my eyes flutter open and I realize that Spot is banging on my bedroom door, trying to get out. He growls and barks loudly, and I sit up and see Papa crack open my door. The house is pitch black, so I know it must still be the middle of the night.

"What's going on?" I mumble sleepily, still feeling the springy cushion of clouds beneath my feet and listening for another thunder clap. Instead, I hear another loud bark.

"I'm going to let Spot out back; he may just need to go potty," Papa says and shushes me back to sleep. As he walks Spot down the hall, however, I hear a loud thud and more barking, followed by a hiss and a wild howl that I've never heard our cats make before.

My eyes shoot open and I stumble out of bed as quickly as I can. Papa grabs onto Spot's collar, pulling him away from my parents' bedroom door and down the stairs. I don't know what's going on. My stomach is in a tight knot.

"Don't hurt him!" I shout as I follow them downstairs.

When I catch up to them, Papa is no longer holding Spot's collar. Spot is standing next to him at the back door, whining. I watch as Papa lets Spot out the door into our backyard.

"Go ahead, Spot, do what you need to do," Papa encourages him and yawns.

Spot wanders around the backyard in the dark, sniffing here and there, before finally deciding on a place behind the tree in the corner of our yard to pee. After that, Spot prances up happily and trots back over to us, wagging his tail.

"Okay, you two, back to bed," Papa declares. But as he pauses to lock the back door, Spot sprints through the living room and back upstairs.

We chase after him, hearing another loud thud as Spot slams against the door, followed by terrified yowls from the cats inside of the bedroom.

"Come on, Spot," Papa urges as he reaches him and grabs his collar, pushing him toward my bedroom. I hear a loud crash from inside of Daddy and Papa's room, followed by some unhappy mumblings from Daddy.

Papa shuts the door to my bedroom after we enter, and Spot bounces up on my bed, lying down with a contented plop at the foot of my bed again.

"Oh, Spot, you've got to leave the cats alone," I say, worry streaking my face. Spot looks up at me and tilts his head to one side, then nuzzles his nose into my hand.

"I think he's trying to protect you because he doesn't know if the cats are a threat or not," Papa explains. "He doesn't know yet that they're part of the family. Let's hope he figures it out soon, for the love of sleep and all of our sanity."

I nod as Papa's mouth stretches into a big yawn, then he leans down and gives me a quick kiss good night and quietly closes the door behind him.

* * *

I am woken up early by the sound of Spot snuffling around my room. I glance at the clock on my bookshelf. I yawn and murmur, "Spot, don't you ever sleep? It's only five in the morning."

Spot turns when he hears me and barks a few happy yips. He prances over and places his front paws on the side of my bed, leaning over to lick at my face.

I laugh and say, "Okay, okay, I get it. You want to wake up. Just one more minute."

Spot hops back down and continues scouting out my room. I doze in and out of sleep, waking a second time to see Spot eating something near my bookshelf. I sit up and lean closer. "Spot, what are you doing?"

Then I see it. I left an open package of dried strawberries on my floor and now Spot is happily chowing down. "Oh, Spot," I moan. Then I sigh and ask, "Are you hungry? All right, let's go downstairs."

Thankfully, Spot trots straight past the cats' bedroom door this time. Daddy and Papa are already downstairs when we get there, sipping tea and reading the newspaper. A plate of scrambled eggs with spinach and red bell peppers is waiting on the counter for me, still warm. Spot's food and water dishes are on the floor, filled to the brim again.

I sit down and vigorously shovel large spoonfuls into my mouth while Spot noisily gulps down his breakfast. I'm always hungrier than normal when I'm tired.

"So the first night didn't go too smoothly," Daddy comments, watching me eat.

Papa looks up and breaks into a big yawn. "And you got to stay in bed during all of the excitement too," he says to Daddy.

"Not all of it. The cats were so afraid of Spot that they tried to jump out of the way to who knows where and ended up knocking over our lamp."

Papa nods and I say, "I heard that! I wondered what that loud crash was. Did it break?"

Daddy shakes his head. "No, but it sure scared the daylights out of the cats and startled me awake."

"Are they still scared now?" I ask through bites of scrambled eggs.

"Nah, lucky ducks are sleeping like angels now," Papa says and smiles. "Maybe we'll let them out to wander around the house later this morning while you and Daddy take Spot on a walk."

"Can Nadine come on the walk with us?" I ask. "I can't wait for her to meet Spot!"

"Sure," Daddy responds. "Why don't you run over there and invite her?"

I put my breakfast plate up on the counter, head

upstairs and quickly brush my teeth and comb my hair, then race over to her house and knock on the door. Her dad answers and right away, I'm bursting with happiness as I tell him my news. "We got a dog! We got Spot! He's at our house right now! Can Nadine come on a walk with us?"

He smiles and says, "That's wonderful! I'm so happy for you. Yes, of course, let me get her."

I step inside and am surrounded by Nadine's dogs, all wagging their tails. I lean over to pet them as Marcelo shouts up the stairs for Nadine.

I look up as Nadine comes flying down the stairs with a thunderous sound, straight into my arms. She wraps her arms around me and gives me the biggest squeeze around my waist. Nadine says goodbye to her dad and follows me back to my house.

I chatter excitedly, my words tumbling over themselves in a rush to get out. I explain all about how amazing it was to get Spot, and about how hard it is for him to get along with the cats.

As we walk in the door, Spot bounds over to us and barks happily.

"Hey, Spot, this is Nadine," I say, introducing them.

Thankfully, Spot doesn't think that I need protecting from Nadine. He sniffs her hand and leans into her, wagging his tail.

"Oh, he's gorgeous, Sophie," she says, kneeling down to pet him. "His fur is so soft and smooth."

Spot stands there patiently, letting her pet him all over.

For the first time since he's been with us, his face breaks into that radiant smile again. My heart explodes with happiness, erasing all of the worries from last night.

* * *

On Monday, I don't want to leave Spot. Papa says he's working from home all week, so he will take care of everything and make sure that Spot and the cats are okay. I reluctantly get ready for school, stopping to give Spot extra hugs and pets before walking out the door.

In class, we are beginning our final end-of-the-year projects. Colby tells us that our class will perform a play based on four of the stories we've read this year. He passes the books around the room—*The Name Jar*, *Thank You, Mr.Falker*, *Each Kindness*, *And Tango Makes Three*. After everyone has had a chance to look through the books again, Colby writes a list of characters on the whiteboard. I sign up to play Unhei from *The Name Jar*. Tino signs up to play Mr. Falker from *Thank You, Mr. Falker*. Emery asks Colby which part is the biggest so he can be on stage the longest.

Immediately, everyone in class is buzzing about their part in the plays. Even Nadine, who is shy about performing in front of people, is excited about playing the part of the baby penguin in *And Tango Makes Three*.

There is a lot to do to prepare for the play. We have costumes and props to choose and background sets to create. Our preparations continue into art class where our art teacher, Rosa, explains that we will spend the rest of our time in art this year preparing for the play. She sets up stations around the classroom filled with different materials.

There's a corner filled with costumes, funny hats, and fun props like giant sunglasses. Big pieces of cardboard and miscellaneous boards of wood are propped up against the wall all along the back of the classroom. One table is set up with paints of every color and paintbrushes bigger than my hand.

Emery rushes over to the costumes and puts on the giant sunglasses. He reaches into the box and pulls out a toy banana, like the kind you'd find in a kitchen play set.

"Don't worry, friends! No one will go hungry here!" he exclaims, waving the banana over his head.

Nadine laughs and dives in, pulling out a toy potato. "Hey, this could be the rock that the penguins sat on before they got an egg," she says and sets it aside.

I smile and turn toward the paints. Looking at the rainbow of colors makes me smile. I feel like anything is possible, like I could paint whatever kind of world I want and it would come true. I walk over to the stack of cardboard at the back of the room and start picturing what I want to create.

Tino joins me and points to a long, curvy piece in front. "Doesn't that kind of look like a dragon?" he asks, pointing.

I nod. "Yes, it does! We could make it into a dragon like the one in the library!" I say excitedly.

"Yeah! And use it for both of our stories!" he says,

giving me a high five.

We place it on top of the art table, then outline the shape of a dragon with a long body and tail. It takes us a long time to cut all the way around the dragon's body. When we finish, Tino pours a deep shade of green onto our palette and we both grab paintbrushes to dip into the paint. Before long, we are both concentrating in silence as the legs and tail slowly turn green. By the time we get to the dragon's neck, Rosa is already telling everyone it's time to clean up.

* * *

When Papa picks me up after school, I get a surprise when I see Spot in the car too. I laugh as Spot sticks his wet nose right against the glass, leaving a smudge above his happy smile.

"Spot!" I exclaim and give him a hug as I climb in the car. "Oh, it's so good to see you!"

Papa hands me a bag of baby carrots as an after-school snack. Spot's nose twitches back and forth, but he stays calmly on his own side and doesn't try to steal my food.

"Good boy," I say, petting his head. "Papa, look how good Spot is! Isn't he a good dog?"

Papa nods as he pulls out of the parking lot. "He sure is, Sophie. We're very lucky to have him. I don't think the cats agree yet, but they'll get there eventually."

Chapter 16

A few days later, I am painting a picture at the table when Daddy bangs the door open and stumbles through, carrying a huge, funny-shaped thing made out of carpet. Spot pops his head up, uncurling himself from the floor where he was sleeping, and races to the front door.

"What is that, Daddy?" I ask, eagerly jumping up and following Spot.

Papa is quicker than I am and has already closed the door behind Daddy, saying, "There you go, set it down right there."

"It's a cat tower, Sophie," Daddy answers, huffing and puffing. "It's so the cats have a place to climb up and stay away from Spot if they need to. Want to help me set it up?"

"Yes!" I exclaim, picking up one side and carrying it down the hall after him.

"You haven't even seen the best part yet," Daddy says, setting the tower in the corner of the living room and handing me a small box that was tucked under his arm. "Check this out. I also got some fun cat hammocks that hang on the wall."

I open the box and pull out the smallest hammocks I have ever seen.

"You hang them up on the wall and the cats can lounge in them like a little bed," he explains.

"Ooh, fun! I want one for me!" I say.

Papa brings us tools as Daddy unfolds the instructions.

Spot sniffs curiously and wiggles closer. Finally, Daddy stretches one hammock several feet above and to the side of the couch.

"We want to hang these low enough that the cats can jump up here easily, but high enough that Spot won't be able to reach them," he explains.

He hands me the electric screwdriver and holds a screw in place for me. It makes a loud whirring noise as it goes in, which makes Spot jump.

We set the tools down and Daddy says, "I think it's time to let the cats out of the bedroom and see how they get along with Spot."

Papa goes into their bedroom first while Daddy hooks Spot's leash onto his collar and brings him upstairs. I wait in the hallway with Daddy and Spot outside the bedroom door. Papa slowly opens the door a crack, barely enough for Spot to stick his paw in. Immediately, Artemis bats at Spot's paw, but she's not growling this time. Artemis pulls her paw back into the bedroom, and Spot flops onto the floor, his bottom still in the air, tail wagging. Spot gives a little whine, and then Orion's paw shoots out from behind the door. Spot jumps up, gives a happy little yip, and presses his nose to the door. Orion bats Spot on the nose and Spot pulls back.

Still, no one is growling and Spot paws at the door again. This time, Papa opens the door a little bit wider and Artemis sticks her head around the door. Her eyes are wide and she's holding completely still, her whole body tense as she stares at Spot.

"Hey, Artemis," Daddy says gently. "This is Spot. What do you think?"

Artemis crouches down low, looking like she's ready to run at any moment. Spot lies down on the floor and rolls over onto his back. He stretches his upside-down head toward Artemis, and Artemis bops him swiftly on the nose again and again. Spot doesn't seem to mind, though, and keeps trying to play.

Finally, Papa pulls the door all the way open and Orion arches his back. His eyes are wide and all of his gray hair is puffed up, making him look like he's twice as big as he normally is. Spot rolls over onto his belly and noses a little closer. Orion stands all the way up on his back two legs, his front paws stuck straight out in the air.

Spot stretches his body all the way out as far as he can, keeping his belly flat on the floor. He sticks his paw out toward Orion, who continues to stand there, staring at him. Artemis walks over and steps right on Spot's head, pressing his ear to the floor, and begins licking Spot's head.

I laugh and say, "Good dog, Spot. See, I told you the cats were nice."

"Oh, that's a good sign," Papa says encouragingly. "They're finally starting to relax around each other."

Orion must be feeling the same way, because he takes advantage of Spot's stillness and inches forward, sniffing at Spot. When Spot flops over, Orion jumps, hisses, bats Spot on the head, and quickly retreats under the bed.

"That's okay," Daddy assures him. "Take your time."

Even though Orion seems to want more space, Artemis looks like she is finally starting to enjoy herself. When she finishes licking Spot's head clean, she rolls over on her back and reaches her front legs up in the air toward Spot, inviting him to play. Spot leans in and gives another happy bark and Artemis jumps up, the wide-eyed look of caution back on her face.

"I think it's going really well, but let's take a little break while I grab one more thing from the car. Come on, Spot," Daddy declares, tugging gently on Spot's leash.

Spot jumps up, tail wagging, and happily trots downstairs.

"What is it, Daddy?" I ask, trailing behind.

"I got a little baby gate like the kind we used when you were little," he explains. "We'll set it up in our bedroom and leave the door open for a while so Spot can see the cats, but they can have space until they're ready to come out."

After we put the baby gate up, Papa unhooks Spot's leash. Spot sits down in the hallway, staring into the bedroom, but he doesn't bark. He sits there patiently, watching the cats inside. Orion is still under the bed and Artemis has moved up on top of the bed and is contentedly purring as she licks her fur. She doesn't seem too concerned about Spot anymore. When she finishes cleaning herself, she turns around in a circle a few times, kneads the blankets, and curls up into a little ball to go to sleep.

* * *

The next week at school, we get to plant the school garden. The afternoon is sunny and warm as we walk outside toward the playground. The garden is made of wood containers filled with dirt that come up to my thighs. Colby says they're called raised garden beds, though that doesn't make any sense to me since you can't sleep in them and gardens don't need sleep anyway.

There are a few long rectangle beds along the back of the garden by the fence, and then the rest are curvy beds that stretch out like snakes toward the playground and picnic tables.

All of our kidney bean plants are sitting in their pots, lined up at the back of the garden. The dirt is dark brown and soft and smells like earth.

"Okay," Colby explains, "grab your plants! We are going to plant the pot and everything today. The pots are made out of compostable cardboard that will dissolve into the soil, so we don't have to transplant them."

I grab a shovel and pick up the light cardboard pot with my name on it. I easily dig a small hole in the soft soil and gently place my pot inside. Then I scoop the soil around the pot, filling the hole in and patting it firmly.

"When you're done planting your kidneys, choose another section of the garden to plant seeds in," Colby shouts.

I look around the rest of the garden beds. Popsicle sticks with names of vegetables written on them poke out of the soil to show where the plants will grow. Next to the popsicle sticks are small packages of seeds.

I open a package of kale seeds and look inside. The package is filled with tiny, chestnut brown seeds.

Nadine opens a package of pumpkin seeds at the other end of the bed and says, "Hey, these look like what I eat when we carve pumpkins and my dad cooks the pumpkin seeds!"

"Really? I want to see!" I say.

Nadine tilts the package closer to me, and as I lean in to see, I accidentally tip the package of kale seeds I was holding, spilling the miniature seeds into the garden.

"Oh no!" I shriek, looking down. Unlike the big, white pumpkin seeds that are easy to see against the dark soil, the kale seeds are so small and dark that it's hard to tell where they all went.

"It's okay, Sophie," Colby says, coming over to us. "Look, there's a big pile of them right here. You don't even have to try to pick them all up. Just grab a shovel from over there and mix the dirt around to spread them out."

"Okay," I say, frowning and holding back tears.

I take a deep breath, mix the seeds into the dirt, and then spread things around as best I can, but I am jealous of Nadine's straight lines and evenly-spaced seeds in her tidy rows.

* * *

Later inside, we continue preparing for the end-of-the-year play. Almost all of the background scenery has been painted, and we are practicing our parts. Nadine gets to be the narrator for my scene since her part as the baby penguin doesn't have many speaking words.

As soon as it's my turn to speak, my hands start to sweat and my breath is shallow and quick. I remembered my words when I was reading them, but now that I'm standing in front of the class and have to say them out loud, I feel like I've just swallowed a big, heavy ball. I start to speak, but my stomach does flip flops and I look down at the floor, not sure what I'm supposed to say next.

Colby steps over and whispers to me, "It's okay, Sophie. Take a big breath. You've got this."

I look up, nod, and breathe in and out slowly. I don't know why it's so much harder to say the words out loud when I love reading and writing so much.

"Would you like me to say your lines first, so you can repeat them?" Colby asks.

I nod and he whispers my lines quietly, and then I repeat them a little louder to the rest of the class. Finally, I'm able to finish practicing my part, and I gratefully sit down. Nadine gives me a little smile and I smile weakly back at her.

Next it's Emery's turn to practice and he hops up eagerly. He says his part loudly and doesn't look nervous at all. In fact, he looks like he's having a lot of fun up in front of the class with all eyes on him. Even when he forgets his line and Colby has to whisper it to him, Emery shouts out his next line with as much energy and confidence as he did before.

* * *

When I get home from school, it is such a relief to see Spot. He greets me at the door and I kneel down and pet him. As I rub my face on his soft fur, my body relaxes and my breathing slows. I nuzzle my face deeper into his neck, then stand up and trudge slowly upstairs.

Spot follows me and sits outside of my parents' bedroom, watching the cats through the baby gate. Artemis is sleeping on the bed, but Orion is sitting on the floor, staring back at Spot. He doesn't growl or hiss, but he makes no move to come closer either. His eyes stay focused on Spot, studying his every move.

I lie down on the floor next to Spot, and he flops down in front of me, curling into me like we are a perfect fit for each other. We both watch Orion through the gate, who just stares back at us.

As I pet Spot, I start to feel better. Maybe it's okay if I'm not the best at the play. Maybe it's okay if I didn't plant the perfect garden today. I lie there on the floor next to Spot and snuggle my nose into his smooth fur and feel glad that he's right there with me. There's nothing better than a sweet dog for comfort after a less-than-perfect day.

Chapter 17

On Saturday, I wake up to the sound of birds singing outside my window. Not just one, little, quiet bird, but so many loud birds that I think there must be a whole flock of birds right outside my window. I sit up and pull my curtains open. Bright sunlight fills my bedroom. I snuggle back into my covers and lie in bed for a few minutes, watching the birds hop from one branch to another on the tree in our backyard. Small, green leaves cover the tree like tiny little dots. I smile and remember how much I love spring days.

I head downstairs for breakfast and see Papa stretched out on the couch, one hand holding a book and the other hand aimlessly stroking Spot's head, which is resting on his thigh. Spot barely raises an eyebrow as I walk by before closing his eyes and resuming his contented snuffling sounds.

"Good morning, sunshine," Papa says. "There's quiche, sweet peas, and strawberries on the counter for you."

"Thanks, Papa," I say, bringing my plate to the table and sitting down. I pour myself a glass of water, only spilling a little bit, and ask, "Where's Daddy? May we go to the dog park with Nadine today?"

"He's outside washing the car, and yes, I think that would be really fun for Spot," Papa replies.

I gobble down my breakfast and rush outside just as

Daddy is about to turn the hose on. The car is covered in soapy bubbles, and the windshield wipers are stuck straight up in the air like giant antennae on a beetle's head.

"May I do it, Daddy? Please?" I shout, running over to him.

"Sure, Sophie, I could use a helper to wash all of the bubbles off," he says, handing me the hose.

I hold the nozzle while he turns the water on. Water shoots out of the hose so fast that it hits the car door in front of me, bounces off the door, and sprays water right in my face.

"Whoa!" I shout, moving the hose to the side and stepping back away from the car. My face and shirt are soaking wet.

Even though it's still morning, the sun is bright and the day is already warm. Being splashed with water feels more refreshing than freezing, and I giggle as I spray down the rest of the car. After a few minutes, the bubbles are gone and water is dripping off the car in fat streams, making puddles on the ground.

"Ooh, good job, Sophie. Look how shiny the windows are now," Daddy praises me as he rolls up the hose. "Would you like to pick up the rags now and toss them in the bucket?"

I shrug and pick up the soapy rags strewn about on the ground and plunk them into the bucket, watching them sink under the fluffy bubbles on top to the dirty, brown water below.

* * *

That afternoon, Daddy finally agrees that we can go to the dog park with Nadine. When we get there, Spot charges through the gate, looking much more awake than he did earlier this morning. He chases Nadine's dogs around in big, happy loops. Nadine throws a tennis ball, and all of the dogs run after it.

Pia runs after the dogs as fast as her chubby, little legs can carry her, shouting, "Mine! Mine!" but she's not fast enough.

Luna, their little white puppy, grabs the ball with her mouth and dashes off. Luna runs in a few big circles around Pia, then drops the ball back by Nadine's feet and zips off with the other dogs again.

Pia races back toward Nadine with her hand outstretched, shouting, "Ball! Ball!"

Nadine looks down at the slimy tennis ball and says, "You can have it, Pia. It's all yours."

Pia reaches for the tennis ball, but before she can pick it up, Spot darts in front of her and steals the ball again. Pia begins chasing the dogs once more, still shouting, "Mine!" after them.

Nadine and I laugh and continue walking around the path that circles the large field. A cool breeze picks up, making goosebumps pop up along my arms. The warmth of the morning is gone, and I wish I'd brought a jacket to put on over my T-shirt.

A dark cloud rolls across the sky, covering the sun, and I shiver, hugging my arms into my sides. Suddenly, a loud crash of thunder echoes across the sky and in an instant, the dogs are racing toward us, eyes wide.

Daddy whistles and Nadine's dad, Marcelo, shouts, "Let's go, kids! Hurry!"

We run to the fence, pausing at the exit only long enough for Daddy and Marcelo to snap leashes on and grab Pia's hand.

"See you!" I shout to Nadine, who is scrambling into her car.

"Bye, Sophie!" she shouts over her shoulder as I fling my door open. Not a moment too soon, as another loud thunder clap booms overhead. Spot shoves me to the side as he barrels into the car, and a heavy downpour of rain cascades over our car.

"Come here, Spot," I coo gently as I climb into my booster and pat my lap. Spot steps onto my lap, leans over to look at the rain streaming down outside, and then dives down again, leaving a smudgy trail from his nose on the window as another thunder clap bursts overhead.

By the time we get home, the rain has turned to hail. It plinks on the roof of our car like popcorn popping on the stove. The sky is dark gray now, lit up momentarily by a flash of lightning, quickly followed by another loud crack of thunder. Spot whines and tries to bury his nose under his paws.

When we pull into our driveway and park, Daddy says, "Hang on a minute, Sophie. Don't open your door until I can get Spot's leash on him. We don't want him running away because he's so scared."

Daddy reaches back from the front seat, hooks the leash onto Spot's collar, and hands the leash to me. As soon as Daddy opens my door, Spot jumps out, his body tense. There is so much hail on the ground that it looks like it's covered in snow. Small, white, pea-sized balls of hail fall from the sky and bounce off the roof onto us. Daddy quickly grabs the leash, and we all scramble up the sidewalk and burst through the front door.

Papa is waiting for us. He has hung a towel over a hook on the wall by the front door and when he hears us enter, he swiftly grabs the towel and bends over to rub Spot all over. Spot's eyes are still wide and his ears are plastered back. He must be so scared that he forgot to shake, and he stands completely still, letting Papa rub him dry. As soon as Papa stands back, though, Spot dashes up the stairs and disappears around the corner.

Next Papa turns to me and hands me a stack of warm, dry clothes. "As soon as I heard that storm rolling in, I knew you'd all be coming home cold and wet. We should have had you take warmer layers with you, but that one kind of snuck up on us."

In dry clothes, but still cold, I follow Papa into the kitchen where hot water is boiling on the stove. "Chamomile or peppermint?"

"Peppermint, please," I say through chattering teeth.

Papa fills mugs of steaming tea and I watch the color steep out of the tea bag, gradually turning the water darker and darker. I breathe in the minty steam rising from my mug and shiver again. When the tea is a dark golden brown, I stir in a small ice cube so I don't burn my tongue. The hot liquid heats me up from the inside out, soothing me.

Papa sips his tea quietly while Daddy lights a fire in the fireplace. Pretty soon, both my belly and the house are toasty warm. The hail has stopped and the rain has calmed to a steady shower. By the time I stand up and set my mug on the counter, a fire is crackling merrily in the fireplace.

"You should have seen Spot, Papa. He was so scared," I say, remembering his wide eyes and fearful whines. "Wait! Where is Spot?"

Daddy looks up and Papa looks around the room. "He must still be upstairs."

I hurry upstairs and search my bedroom, then search my parents' office. No Spot. I even check in the upstairs bathroom. Still no Spot. I shoot back downstairs, calling for Spot. "Is he here? He's not upstairs!"

Daddy and Papa stand up and quickly search the room.

"Last time I saw him, he was going upstairs," Papa says, heading toward the stairs.

I follow Daddy and Papa as they search my bedroom, the office, and the bathroom again. Still no Spot and no response to our calls. Finally, they swing the baby gate open and step into their bedroom. I follow, but I don't see any animals anywhere. Now that I think about it, I haven't seen the cats either since we've been home.

Papa gets down on his hands and knees, pushes the comforter aside, and looks under their bed as Daddy flicks the light on. "Well, well . . . what have we here?"

I crouch down next to him and look under their bed. Spot is curled up in a corner with Artemis and Orion snuggled right next to him. All three of them stare back at us with wide eyes. None of them are moving or making a sound. They are so close together that if it were any darker, I wouldn't have been able to tell them apart. It took a crazy storm, thunder, and hail to do it, but they have finally become a family.

Chapter 18

The next day, we take Spot back to the animal shelter to volunteer at their Earth Day event. We go straight to the outdoor play area where the sun is shining and the dogs are running around barking happily. Spot paws the ground and whines, tugging on his leash. "Hang on there, Spot," Papa tells him, bending over to unhook his leash.

The minute the leash is off, Spot charges forward and runs in big, happy loops with the other dogs. I look around and see Hayes over by the fence throwing a ball for the skinniest dog I've ever seen. Its face is narrow and its legs are tall and slender.

I head over, bending down to pet the dog's soft, mottled fur. "Oh my gosh, it is so skinny! And its fur is so soft!"

"I know. It's a greyhound. Watch this," Hayes responds. He stands up and throws a tennis ball up in the air. The greyhound leaps into the air and tries to catch the ball, which bounces off its nose and rolls across the grass. Without missing a beat, the dog chases after it, running and diving faster than any dog I've ever seen.

I hear a familiar voice and turn to see Jazmin and her bright, friendly smile. "May I have your attention, please? Thank you all for coming. We've been doing this Earth Day celebration here at Lucky Dog Animal Shelter for five years now. So grab a pooch, a garbage bag, and either a trash-picker-upper stick or some plastic gloves, and let's head out to clean up our trail."

Hayes leashes up the puppy while I call for Spot. Daddy and Papa walk over toward us with a pit bull and a collie on leashes. "You guys ready? We've got everything we'll need."

Hayes and I nod and head out of the gate, turning toward the trail. The greyhound tries to sniff everything in sight, pulling Hayes this way and that. Spot walks calmly by my side, stopping to wait for me when I find trash on the ground to add to Daddy's garbage bag. Daddy's collie sniffs the garbage bag and snuffles loudly, but pulls his head back when Daddy tells him firmly, "That's not for you, bud."

A cool breeze floats gently over us, ruffling the leaves in the trees and making goosebumps break out across my skin. But the sun stays out, only partially hidden by soft, white clouds that pass quickly across the sky.

We settle into an enjoyable, quiet mood, punctuated only by the sudden bursts of energy as the collie zigzags Daddy across the trail in search of a squirrel or flower. The way his nose moves constantly, you'd think the trail smelled like our kitchen on Thanksgiving. The only thing I smell is a faint scent of damp earth and fresh flowers.

By the end of the afternoon, we've filled our little garbage bag halfway with trash, and many of the other groups have too. Daddy tosses our bag into the big garbage bin outside, and we bring the dogs back inside.

Jazmin thanks everyone for coming, and we stroll down the hallway back out toward the main lobby. As we pause to say goodbye to Hayes, I glance at the wall and see a photo of me and Spot hanging in a frame. I have a broad smile across my face and my arms around Spot's neck.

I decide that I want to keep volunteering here even though we've already adopted Spot. Maybe someday I'll work here when I grow up. Or maybe I'll be a vet. I think that would be cool.

* * *

Now that things have calmed down at home, we don't need the baby gate anymore. Spot plays with Artemis and Orion in the living room until the cats get tired of him and jump up onto the cat hammocks, relaxing from their safe perch. The weeks fly by in a swirl of easy comfort at home and final preparations for the play at school.

The days are getting warmer, too, so as I dress for school one morning, I only need a tank top and shorts. As we finish up breakfast in class that morning, our art teacher, Rosa, joins Colby at the front of the classroom.

Colby explains, "You get a choice for your year-end project. You may either stay here and write about your favorite things from this year, or you may follow Rosa to the art room and create an art project to represent your favorite things from this year."

Nadine and Tino quickly file into a line with about half of the students in our class, but I stay in my seat. Emery is still sitting in his seat too. I love art, but my favorite thing is writing. After Rosa leads the students back to the art room, Colby asks for a volunteer to hand out the writing journals. My hand shoots up in the air. "Thank you, Sophie. Here you go," Colby says, handing me a stack of journals.

After I pass out all of the journals, I sit down and Colby asks us to start brainstorming. I love this part. I always think of a thunder and lightning storm going on in my brain. "All right, who remembers what we did when school first started?"

Emery's hand shoots up and he says, "We got to have P.E. outside and I found a bunch of crickets!"

Colby writes "P.E. outside" and "crickets" on the board.

I add, "And we got to play with Maddie in math."

Colby adds "Maddie in math" and says, "Good. What are some of your favorite memories from this year?" He continues to write as other kids add things like "habitat report," "lunch," "recess," and "fire station field trip."

Eventually, the board is filled up and Colby says, "I think we've got enough things to get started. Go ahead and start writing. Remember to use fun words and all five senses to describe what's happening."

I don't even have to think about what I'm going to write about. I start by writing about how wonderful it was to have Maddie in math class, and how much easier it was to learn math with her in the room. Then I start writing about volunteering at the animal shelter over winter break. And, of course, meeting Spot and finally bringing him home. I know not all of it happened at school, but it was this year, so I decide that it's okay to include.

Pretty soon Colby says, "Okay, time to wrap it up. You'll have more time later if you need to finish. We're going to display your journals at our end-of-the-year celebration when you perform your play."

* * *

The next week is the last week of school, which means that our end-of-the-year celebration is finally here. I'm standing backstage, dressed in a green shirt and brown pants like Unhei from *The Name Jar*. I listen to Nadine read the narrator's part. My breath comes in shallow, quick gasps. I stare down at the ground, wishing I were home with Spot.

Finally, it's my turn and I step out onto stage. I glance into the audience and see Daddy giving me a thumbs-up and Papa waving at me, smiles on their faces. I take a deep breath and smooth my hands on my thighs, trying to stay calm.

"I just moved here from Korea . . ." I start.

One line leads into another, and I keep going. My breath continues in quick, shallow bursts between words. I feel my cheeks turning hot and red. At one point, I forget the next line.

I look over to Colby, who's standing offstage, and he calmly whispers to me, "My name means grace."

I repeat, "My name means grace." And suddenly I remember the next line. And the line after that. Finally, my scene is done and I rush backstage.

Emery is up next and his voice is loud and sure. He is

beaming as he talks, and he's full of energy as he moves around the stage. I feel a little better seeing how happy he is standing up on stage, but I'm still relieved when the play is over. Everyone claps and Emery takes the biggest bow of all. He is smiling from ear to ear.

Next Colby takes the stage and announces, "Please join us outside now. We have a little party to celebrate everything we've accomplished this year."

I find Daddy and Papa in the audience, wiggle my way in between them, and hold both of their hands as we all walk outside to the playground. Tables are lined up between the garden and the playground, displaying the journals and artwork that we made to show our favorite part of the year.

"Look, Daddy, here's my journal," I say, pointing to a notebook with two dogs drawn on the front. One is a yellow lab like Maddie, and the other is a big, brown dog with a white spot on its chest like Spot.

"I could have guessed that was yours," he replies and smiles.

Next to us, Emery is reading a story to his parents about a frog in a swamp. At the next table, Tino is showing his dad a painting of himself on a fire truck. I can hear him talking about how fun it was climbing up into the big fire engine and how it felt like flying when he jumped down. I smile, remembering that's exactly what I thought too!

At another table, Nadine is holding up little people that she made next to a ceramic house. I watch as she bends down and holds out the smallest figure to Pia. I lean closer and hear her say, "See, Pia, this one is you. You're the smallest one in our family. Do you want to keep it?" Pia nods eagerly and wraps her tiny hand around the figure.

Colby steps over to me and gives me a high five. "Good job in the play, Sophie! I know you were nervous, but you did really well."

"Thanks," I reply, still glad that it's over. "I don't remember what I said at all."

"Well, you sounded very strong and confident," Daddy assures me.

"When I'm really nervous, I won't remember exactly what I did or said later either," Papa tells me.

I'm just glad it's over. Next year, I think I'll see if I can only do the props so I don't have to say anything. Or maybe I can be something that doesn't talk. That might be okay.

"Only two more days and you'll be a fourth grader," Colby says, smiling. "Are you ready?"

I nod eagerly.

Daddy declares, "I know she's ready, but I don't know if I am quite yet. Sometimes it all goes a little too fast for me."

I look up to see Daddy wiping the corners of his eyes.

Papa reaches out and rubs Daddy's back. "I know what you mean."

We walk by the garden before we leave. Nadine's pumpkin seeds have sprouted and are already turning into the cutest green plants all lined up in a perfectly straight line and spaced evenly apart.

Next to them, I notice a big bunch of dark green, curly leaves where I spilled the kale seeds. They're growing like a thick, overgrown jungle, each plant fighting to get to the top. I guess they turned out all right.

I take Daddy and Papa over to our kidney bean plants and am surprised at how tall they are. Most of the plants have a lot of leaves on them now. Some are even starting to form the beginnings of flowers, but none of them have bloomed yet. They are all still growing.

* * *

On the last day of school, our classroom buzzes with students laughing and joking. The energy of summer fills the air. Colby has taken down our schoolwork and artwork. The bare walls remind me of a skeleton—empty and kind of lonely. The table along the back of the classroom is piled high with notebooks, papers, and projects. Emery and Nadine get to hand them out to everyone while the rest of us pull our backpacks from our cubbies.

In a rush, we cram everything into our backpacks. I have so much stuff that it won't all fit, so I shove as many notebooks into my backpack as I can and then balance a stack of papers in my arms and line up by the door. When Daddy picks me up, he smiles and takes the papers from me as I bounce eagerly into his arms.

"Hey, sweetie," he says, taking my heavy backpack too. "Can you believe you're done with third grade already?"

I smile. Third grade was the best year ever, because my

biggest wish finally came true. I think about how hard it was to wait for Spot and how some days, it felt like everyone else in the whole world would get a dog except me. I think back and realize that the whole time I was waiting for Spot, he was waiting for us to adopt him. It was hard to be patient, but Spot was worth the wait. Now that we have Spot, it's hard to imagine my life without him.

"I knew it was going to be a good year, Daddy."

ACKNOWLEDGMENTS

First and foremost, I am indebted to Aiden Byers for providing me with the inspiration from which this story was born. And for naming the book, listening to me read early drafts, reading the beta version, and advising me on the plot, characters, and placement of commas. I am so grateful that we were able to share this experience and I hope we collaborate on many more books together in the future.

Sometimes you don't get up and chase after your dreams until you see someone else chasing theirs. Jean Lowe Carlson was the one who sparked my enthusiasm and inspired me to become a self-published author, instead of just dreaming about it. Thank you.

Back when I was a burnt-out attorney with only a dream of writing, I fortuitously stumbled upon the Writers Idea Factory. You all welcomed me with open arms and accepted me exactly where I was—which happened to be exhausted and pessimistic. Your acceptance was the cocoon that enabled me to transform into someone who is now energized and hopeful. Thank you for being there when I needed you most.

This book could have ended up in the scrap pile were it not for the gentle reassurance of Sarah Dodson-Knight. Thank you for reading my nearly-complete first draft and instilling in me the confidence to continue. Your thoughtful criticism sandwiched between specific compliments and positive encouragement was exactly what I needed to hear. Thank you.

My critique partners, Lynne Aseret, Taylor Morris, and Ron Quintana provided valuable insight to develop this story by thoughtfully analyzing my writing, paying close attention to every word and phrase I wrote, and suggesting places that could be improved. In addition, you played a crucial role in my journey as a writer by helping build my confidence enough to share my stories with the world. Thank you.

I chose a team of beta readers who represented different aspects of my book that I wanted to preview before I sent it out into the world. I am eternally grateful to elementary school librarian David Smith for his careful reading and constructive comments on how to improve the story and subplots. Thank you for pointing out that penguins don't live in the Arctic, for discussing which books third graders read, and for advising me about my price point and target audience. You have been an incredible resource; thank you a million times over!

Thank you to third grade teacher Maria Comparini for generously sharing your expertise to confirm that Sophie's schoolwork and classroom assignments were age appropriate, and that this is a book that third graders will want to read.

Thank you to Abigale and Dandelion Grace for your valuable feedback about the introduction of Daddy and Papa, and for brainstorming ways to show some gay pride.

A very special thank-you to my children beta readers: Kaliyah Schimpf, Lucia Dale, Naima Ponti, Judah White, and Elliot. I am so grateful for your enthusiasm and willingness to jump right in and share your thoughts about my book. I loved reading your comments and seeing this story through your eyes.

Even talented writers and editors make mistakes in their manuscripts, and I am no exception. Thank you to Taylor Morris, Debbie Rohlfs, Kathleen Byers, and Jean Lowe Carlson for proofreading my book before publication. I am still amazed at all of the different typos that each of you found, and my book is so much better because of your careful corrections.

Having a cover made me realize that I didn't just write some words; I wrote a book! Patty Kelly was the one who made sure that my cover was exactly the way I wanted it to be—exceptional. Thank you for the many hours we devoted to this project, tweaking everything until it was exactly right. Your patience and design skills are invaluable to me in equal measure.

Penny Weber was the artist who illustrated Sophie and Spot. Thank you for bringing Sophie's joyfulness to life. You captured her cheerfulness and optimism perfectly, and Spot is just the way I imagined him.

Lastly, to my husband, Kyle, you have been there through all of it. I owe you about a million dollars for your never-ending tech support, accounting services, and business advice. Your beta reader comments were insightful and helped me correct all of the places where characters magically appeared in the middle of a scene. Most importantly, though, I am so grateful that you chose to share this journey with me, even when it felt like a roller coaster.

50435975R10114

Made in the USA
Columbia, SC
07 February 2019